A Cornucopia of Murder

A Charlie Kingsley Mystery

Books by Michele Pariza Wacek
MPWNovels.com/books

Secrets of Redemption series:
It Began With a Lie (Book 1)
This Happened to Jessica (Book 2)
The Evil That Was Done (Book 3)
The Summoning (Book 4)
The Reckoning (Book 5)
The Girl Who Wasn't There (Book 6)
The Room at the Top of the Stairs (Book 7)
The Search (Book 8)
The Secret Diary of Helen Blackstone (novella)

Charlie Kingsley Mystery series:
A Grave Error (prequel novella)
The Murder Before Christmas (Book 1)
Ice Cold Murder (Book 2)
Murder Next Door (Book 3)
Murder Among Friends (Book 4)
The Murder of Sleepy Hollow (Book 5)
Red Hot Murder (Book 6)
A Cornucopia of Murder (Book 7)
A Room for Murder (Book 8)
A Wedding to Murder For (novella)
Loch Ness Murder (novella)

The Redemption Detective Agency series:
The Mysterious Case of the Missing Motive (Book 1)

Stand-a-lone books:
The Taking
The Third Nanny
Mirror Image
The Stolen Twin
Today I'll See Her (novella)

A Cornucopia of Murder

A Charlie Kingsley Mystery

by Michele Pariza Wacek

For more information, contact Michele Pariza Wacek,
PO Box 10430 Prescott, AZ 86304.
info@LoveBasedPublishing.com.

ISBN 978-1-945363-71-9

Library of Congress Control Number: 2023950238

For my family, for always believing in me.

Chapter 1

"Hi Nancy," I said, tucking the phone between my ear and shoulder as I bent down to pull the freshly baked pumpkin pie out of the oven. The pecan pie I had baked earlier was cooling on the counter, and the kitchen smelled of sugar, cinnamon and pumpkin. Midnight, my black cat, was snoozing in his favorite chair, which was positioned right next to the window so the sun would slant across him. "You'll be happy to know the pies are baked and cooling."

"Hey Charlie," Nancy said, her voice hesitant. "Glad to hear it. And, well, that's what I was calling about,"

I paused, one hand on the handle of the open oven door. Although I had turned the oven off, the heat was still wafting up toward my face, and I could feel the sweat start to bead on my forehead. "Is there a problem?" I wondered if she was calling to cancel her annual Thanksgiving dinner, which would mean no turkey for me. On the flip side, I would have plenty of pie to eat.

Nancy owned the Redemption Inn, and every year she hosted a small Thanksgiving dinner at the hotel for a handful of us who had no family in the area, plus any hotel guests who also had nowhere to go for the holiday. I had been a regular for Thanksgiving since I first moved to Redemption, Wisconsin a few years back.

"I'm not sure," Nancy said. "How many pies did you make?"

"Two," I said. "One pecan and one pumpkin."

"Only two?"

I ran a hand through my brownish, blondish hair, damp with sweat from the heat of the kitchen, and took a step back from the oven. I was sure my cheeks were bright red. "Was I supposed to make more? I thought we agreed that two would be enough. There are eight of us, right?"

"Well, actually, I think there's going to be eleven now," Nancy said.

"Eleven?" I studied the pies. If there were going to be eleven of us, then we all couldn't have a piece of pumpkin pie. Did I have enough pumpkin to make another pie? "How did we get to eleven?"

"Well, there's you and me," Nancy said, "and Pat and Richard." Pat was my best friend, and Richard was her husband. Normally they would be celebrating Thanksgiving with their daughter, but she was spending Thanksgiving with her boyfriend's family, so Nancy had invited them to join us. "And Tilde. You know Tilde, right?"

"Of course I know Tilde," I said, trying to keep the sigh out of my voice. Tilde was a retired nurse who had now decided to start a second career as a private investigator, and she had chosen me as her mentor. I, unfortunately, didn't have much to say about it. Hopefully, I wasn't going to be spending the entire Thanksgiving meal answering questions about the sleuthing business, especially since I didn't even consider myself a sleuth. I was a tea maker—I grew herbs and flowers in my backyard and turned them into custom teas that I sold out of my house. The sleuthing part was a side benefit for any tea client who found themselves in a bit of a pickle with the law, which was a lot more of them than you might imagine.

I never expected to be a sleuth, much less have a knack for it. Most of the time I had no idea what I was doing, which made Tilde's questions... uncomfortable.

Hopefully, she would decide Thanksgiving was an excellent time to take a break from her "mentoring."

This would be Tilde's first Thanksgiving, at least since I had been attending. Tilde was active in the Redemption community and had many friends, plus she had a sister who lived elsewhere, Riverview I think, who she would sometimes see over the holidays. They were more or less estranged, but Tilde still made an effort, as she was close to her niece. I wasn't sure why all her normal plans fell through this year, but regardless, Nancy had invited her.

"Oh, that's right," Nancy said. "I remember Tilde mentioning something about you being her mentor in her new side gig."

I closed my eyes. This was going to be fun. "So, that's five, and you had two guests joining us as well, right? Or are there more?"

"No, it's still only two. Both single men with no families back home, so it made no sense for them to leave for Thanksgiving."

"Okay, we're up to seven, if my math is right. And Ginny is going to be there again, right? So that makes eight." Like me, Ginny had been a fixture at Nancy's Thanksgiving get-togethers. Also, like me, the reason why she was there was because she was more or less estranged from her family, although she would never say it like that. She had three adult children who all seemed to be way too busy with their own lives to make time for her at Thanksgiving.

"Yes, Ginny is going to be there." The hesitation was back in Nancy's voice. "Along with her three kids."

I paused, not sure I heard correctly. "Ginny is coming with all three kids? Why would she do that? If they're all here, why doesn't she have Thanksgiving at her house?"

Nancy let out a long, deep sigh. "It's complicated. So Elias? He's the eldest and normally has a quiet Thanksgiving at home with his wife and kids. Except he got divorced this year. It was very messy and painful, but I guess the plan was he was still going to be there for Thanksgiving. For the kids' sake. They're trying to keep things normal or ... something for them." Her voice held a skeptical tone. "Anyway, he and his ex had a dreadful fight a couple of weeks ago and that was it for Thanksgiving, so he called Ginny to see what her plans were, and of course she told him to come home. Then she called me and asked if it would be okay if she brought him as well. She didn't feel up to doing a huge Thanksgiving meal for just her and Elias, so I said absolutely." She paused and her voice sounded almost embarrassed. "I didn't call to tell you, because it was just one more person, so I figured two pies would be fine."

"Two pies would have been fine," I said.

"Okay, so we were up to nine. But then, a couple of days ago, Ginny calls back a second time and apparently her daughter Miriam was going to be joining them for Thanksgiving. Miriam travels a lot for her job. She's some high-powered executive. Always flying to Europe and Asia. Anyway, she's rarely home for the holidays. She's rarely home at all. But I guess it was a last-minute cancellation, so she called and asked Ginny if it would be okay if she came home for Thanksgiving. Of course Ginny said yes, and then ..."

"Ginny called you," I said.

"I was going to call," Nancy said, her voice now sounding a little pleading. "I figured even with ten people, two pies would be okay, but we've been so busy, just crazy busy, and Lee has been home sick with the flu, and it's been a zoo. I completely lost track of time."

"It's okay," I said. "I don't expect you to run everything by me. And ten people and two pies isn't a big deal."

"Well, Ginny was very apologetic as well," Nancy said. "She said it was still only the three of them, and she only had a couple of days to prepare, but if it was going to be too much hassle, she would have figured it out, but I told her 'nonsense', and that we'd be happy to have both of them."

"And you were right to do it," I said. "I would have said exactly the same thing."

"Oh, that's what I thought you would say," Nancy said, her voice sounding more relieved. "I know ten is cutting it a little close. I mean, if it wasn't Thanksgiving, two pies would be plenty, but you know everyone is going to want a second piece. Especially since your pies are so good."

"Flattery will get you everywhere," I said, opening the fridge to see if I had enough ingredients for more pies or if I was going to have to also make a quick run to the store, and fight all the other last minute shoppers who had forgotten some important item. "So, what's the story of the third child?"

"That would be Caleb and … that's kind of a strange one." Her voice changed, sounded more pensive. "He's the black sheep, you know."

I shut the refrigerator door, my attention perking up. "Black sheep?"

"Oh, that's right. I keep forgetting you haven't lived here all that long. Caleb left Redemption the moment he turned eighteen and has never been back."

Now I was definitely intrigued. "Never?"

"Not to my knowledge."

"Why not?"

"I'm not sure about the details. There was some … unpleasantness while he was in high school. If I remember correctly, he was expelled over it."

"Expelled?" My jaw dropped. "And you don't remember why?" Redemption being a small town, with gossip being its main currency, I was having trouble believing that.

"They tried to keep it kind of hush hush, out of respect for Ginny. She was always such a pillar of the community. Plus, Elias and Miriam were always such good kids, no one wanted whatever Caleb got mixed up in to rub off on them. I do remember he was bad news, always getting into trouble. It may have all just gotten too much, and they expelled Caleb. But I think there was something more, something no one wanted to talk about much. Or, at least, no one who might know something. And once he left, that was kind of the end of it."

"That makes it sound like there was some major issue," I said. "Otherwise, why wouldn't he have come back?"

"I don't know the whole story, but it seems like Caleb didn't get along with his siblings," Nancy said. "At least, that's how Ginny explains it every time it comes up. Although she doesn't like to talk about it much. I get the feeling she really misses Caleb."

As a fellow black sheep, I could commiserate with Caleb's situation. I, too, rarely went home as it typically ends up being an unpleasant experience for everyone, but I was still in touch with my family. I regularly spoke to my sister Annabelle, even if some of the calls were … chilly. To have no contact at all for years seemed to indicate this was more than just lots of 'getting in trouble' incidents.

And if that was the case, why would he come back now?

"I don't know," Nancy said when I asked her. "Ginny didn't say. She sounded flustered when I called. I got the impression Caleb just sort of … showed up."

"He didn't call or write?"

"Like I said, she didn't get into specifics, but it sure sounded like he rang the doorbell this morning and when she answered, there he was."

"This morning?" No wonder why Ginny seemed flustered, and why Nancy sounded so apologetic.

"I know, I know. So, of course, now it's really too late for Ginny to try and cobble together a Thanksgiving meal, which leads me back to the pies …"

"I can make another pie," I said quickly, even though I wasn't looking forward to the mad dash to the grocery store. "It's no problem."

"Oh, thank you." Nancy's voice came out in a rush, as if she was holding her breath this entire time. "I know this is a lot to ask …"

"Truly, it's not a problem. I'm happy to help."

"Great. So do you think three pies will be enough, or do you think we need four?"

It was pretty obvious what answer Nancy wanted to hear. "I can make two more pies."

"Oh, perfect. So, the dessert is taken care of. Now I just have to make sure Tilde is bringing enough stuffing and Pat is bringing enough green bean casserole. And then I have to get back into the kitchen and start the rolls and the mashed potatoes, at least the turkey is in the oven."

"I can talk to Pat," I said, taking the hint.

"Oh, would you? That would save me a lot of time. I'll just give Tilde a quick jingle, but she's probably made enough for an army as it is."

"No problem at all," I said. "I'll give her a call right now." That way, if Pat needed something from the store, I could add that to my shopping list. No sense both of us wasting time running to the store.

Chapter 2

"Caleb is here?" Pat repeated for what seemed like the tenth time.

"And you're going to be able to talk to him in person unless I'm not able to get my pies baked in time," I said, adjusting the phone that was tucked between my chin and shoulder and jotting down another note for myself. As soon as I hung up with Nancy, I had called Pat. I figured if she needed more ingredients from the store to make another green bean casserole, I could pick them up for her rather than both of us having to suffer the holiday crowds.

"It's just ... I didn't think he would ever be back."

I put the pencil down I was holding. "Why? What did he do? Nancy didn't know."

"Of course Nancy knows," Pat scoffed. "She probably doesn't want to talk about it. It was a horrible scandal, and Ginny didn't deserve any of it."

"*What* was?"

"Murder."

"*Murder*?" I nearly dropped the phone. "Caleb killed someone?"

"That was the rumor at the time," Pat said. "Although no one knows for sure. It was definitely hushed up."

"How can murder be hushed up? Wasn't there a trial? Didn't he go to jail?"

"Well, that's the thing. He was underage, as was the kid he allegedly killed. But nothing was ever confirmed."

"What do you mean, nothing was ever confirmed?"

Pat sighed. "You have to keep in mind, this was over twenty years ago. Things were different back then. The school officials claimed there was not a crime. It was just a prank that had gone very wrong."

I couldn't believe what I was hearing. "But someone died. Even if it was a prank that had gone wrong, someone needs to be held accountable."

"But that's the thing. Everyone said there was no crime. The kid, the one who had been supposedly killed, was still alive."

I glanced at the clock. I really didn't have time for this. I needed to get to the store and get the pies in the oven. But I also couldn't bring myself to hang up the phone. "I don't understand. If the kid was still alive, then how is Caleb a murderer?"

"That's why it was such a scandal," Pat said. "The kid, I wish I could remember his name. Was it Dick or John or … ? No, that's not right. I can't remember. Anyway, even though all the officials said he was still alive, no one could confirm they had actually seen him alive. He just … vanished."

"Vanished," I said, a cold pit forming in my stomach. It was not uncommon for people to vanish in Redemption, Wisconsin, and I was already getting a bad feeling about where this was going.

"Exactly," Pat said, her tone echoing my thoughts. "They said he had transferred to another school but wouldn't say which school. And his mother — if I remember correctly he was raised by a single mother — she had also disappeared. Quit her job and just up and left Redemption. Didn't respond to calls, just … vanished. Why would she do that if it was just a prank, and her son had simply transferred to another school?"

"Good question," I said. "It sure does seem like a cover up. But why? Did Ginny have money or something so she could bribe people?"

"Not to my knowledge. She did fine, don't get me wrong, but they weren't rich, or if they were, they sure didn't act like it. But she was considered a pillar of society and a lot of people respected her. I know some people were loath to talk about Caleb because they didn't want to hurt Ginny."

Nancy had said the same thing. Was it possible that even if Ginny didn't have money, she had power, and that's why her son's involvement in this scandal was covered up?

I pictured Ginny. She had always struck me as the grandmother type, with her helmet of tight, blue-rinsed curls, gold-rimmed glasses, plump body and smiling face. It was hard to picture her as someone who would have been ruthless enough to have covered up her son's crime, especially if he truly was guilty of murder. But I also knew it would be a mistake to underestimate a mother's love for her child.

"And, of course, it's Redemption," Pat said. "It's not like it's that uncommon for people to disappear here."

"Yes, but you have to admit, that would be a wild coincidence," I said. "He just happened to disappear at a time when he could have been murdered?"

"You know how it is," Pat said. "Stranger things have happened."

While true, I thought in this case it was stretching even Redemption's history of bizarre happenings.

Back in 1888, all the adults disappeared, leaving only the children. No one knew what had happened to them, including the children. They had claimed the adults were there one day and gone the next.

Ever since that fateful day, strange occurrences—things like disappearances, hauntings and murder--had plagued Redemption. Far more than should be happening in a town of its size.

On the surface, Redemption appeared to be a small, charming, wholesome, midwestern town located in Southern Wisconsin, nestled in-between forests, lakes and farmlands.

But, nothing was ever as it seemed. Especially in Redemption.

So, while it was certainly possible that the kid simply vanished just because he had the bad luck to live in Redemption, it was also possible there was something more sinister going on.

I glanced at the clock again. Yikes, I was going to be cutting it close. "So back to Thanksgiving. Did you need anything from the store, or do you think you have enough green bean casserole?"

"It's a pretty big casserole," Pat said. "Bringing a second one seems a little much, but I could bring a salad. I have enough lettuce and tomatoes, plus a few other veggies like carrots, but I could use some cucumbers and peppers, if you wouldn't mind picking those up for me."

"I can do that," I said, even though I wasn't sure how popular salad would be for Thanksgiving. If we were short on food, it would at least be something of a filler.

"I doubt we're going to have any issues with food," Pat said. "Richard isn't going to be there."

"He's not? Why?"

"You don't want to know," Pat said darkly. "I think it's food poisoning, but let's just say he hasn't left the bathroom much today."

"Oh. Yeah, I guess Thanksgiving is not something he would be all that interested in."

"No, not at all, and he's not happy about it. He loves a good Thanksgiving meal. I promised him I'd see if I could sweet-talk Nancy into leftovers. You, too. He was especially looking forward to your pies."

"He absolutely can have some pie," I said, "and let him know if there is nothing left over, I'll make him one."

"Oh, I wouldn't dream of telling him that," Pat said. "I'm trying to keep him on a diet."

As I knew Pat also enjoyed her desserts, I wasn't sure how hard either one of them was trying to diet.

"Speaking of pies, what kinds are you making?" Pat tried to keep her voice casual, but I wasn't fooled.

"Well, right now I have pumpkin and pecan," I said. "I haven't decided what the other two pies should be."

"Oh, I love a good pecan pie," Pat said. "You can never go wrong with pecan."

"I could, but it is Thanksgiving, and pecan pies are kind of rich. Don't you think another pumpkin pie would make sense?"

"True," Pat said. "I guess you could also do something like apple as well."

"Apple would work," I said thoughtfully.

"Or what about a nice lemon meringue pie?" Pat's voice had a note of longing in it. Lemon meringue was Pat's favorite pie.

"That's not really a traditional Thanksgiving pie," I said.

"You could start a new tradition," Pat said.

I shook my head. "Tell you what. Once Richard is better, I will make you and Richard a lemon meringue pie."

"Ack, don't do that," Pat yelped. "He'll gobble it down and I'll be lucky to get a piece."

"I guess I'll make two pies then," I said. At this rate, I was hoping I would make it through the holiday season without being completely sick of making pies.

Chapter 3

"Are you ready for this?" I asked Pat. I had just pulled into the parking lot of the Redemption Inn. Even though it was located in downtown Redemption, you wouldn't know it by looking at it. Surrounded by tall pines and majestic oak trees, it was like spending time in a log cabin in the woods. Albeit a giant log cabin, but still a cabin.

Normally it felt warm and homey visiting, but not today, Today it had an ominous look to it, like we were visiting a house trapped in the middle of nowhere, although that might have been because the weather was starting to turn threatening. The wind had picked up, whistling through the bare trees, and the sky was a menacing slate gray.

Pat was sitting next to me with Tiki, her toy poodle, on her lap. They were dressed in matching orange sweaters, although Tiki had a colorful turkey on hers, along with orange ribbons by her ears. Tiki also looked far more excited to be there than her owner, as the little dog's tail was wagging furiously while Pat's brow was furrowed.

"I think so," she said, although she didn't sound convinced. "I'm still trying to decide if this is going to be a really interesting evening or a massive mistake."

"Yeah, witnessing the first day a black sheep decides to come home may be more volatile than we want to deal with."

"Exactly," Pat said, her frown deepening. She was a good decade or so older than me and the best way to describe her was round. She was plump, with a round face, round black-rimmed glasses, and short, no-nonsense brown hair that was turning gray.

I shivered. I needed to get a grip, or I was going to end up driving back home and forgetting about turkey.

Pat must have sensed my mood because she gave me a knowing look. "I guess we ought to go in, huh? No sense sitting out here in a cold car."

I unbuckled my seat belt. "No, I guess not."

It took a bit of a balancing act but, between the two of us, we managed to carry all four pies, the green bean casserole, salad, and toy poodle to the front door. The wind tugged at my coat, as if it was trying desperately to get my attention.

"Oh, I almost forget to ask, what kind of pie did you end up making?" Pat asked.

"Mincemeat," I said.

Pat's eyes went wide. "Seriously? It's been ages since I had a good mincemeat pie."

"Yeah, that's what I was thinking. It might be a nice change."

"So, you have mincemeat, pecan, and …"

"Two pumpkins," I said as we stepped onto the large front porch.

"Oh, man, what do we need dinner for? We could just eat pie," Pat said. She smiled as she said it so I would know she was joking, but only partly.

"Don't tempt me," I said as I stared at the doorknob, wondering how I was going to be able to open the door or if I was going to need to put the pies down. I didn't need to have worried because, at that moment, the door flung open, revealing Nancy.

"Oh, good, you made it. I was starting to worry. Here, let me help you out with those," she said as she took two of the pies from me. She tried to take the third one, but I waved her back and she ended up taking a dish from Pat. Despite being older than both of us, Nancy somehow was always able to carry more than both of us combined.

"Well, hello there cutie," she said to Tiki, who gave her a kiss on the nose. Nancy laughed. "You're very festive."

"So are you," I said. Nancy wore a black sweater covered with pictures of pumpkins, squash, and multi-colored corn. Her ever-present gold glasses hung on a chain that dangled over her ample bosom and seemed to complete the ensemble.

She smiled. "Isn't it great? I saw it and had to have it."

"It's perfect for you," I said, as it occurred to me that her hair, over-permed and over-dyed, was the perfect match for the corn. Actually, even more than the color, the texture seemed to match the dried stalks on her sweater as well.

She craned her neck, as if trying to look behind Pat. "Where's Richard? Is he getting more stuff out of the car?"

"He had terrible food poisoning and had to stay home," Pat said.

"Oh, poor guy, I'll have to send some turkey home with you," she said absentmindedly as she examined the food she was holding. "You still made four pies, didn't you?" She sounded a little more panicked than I thought was warranted.

"I did," I said.

"And I brought a salad along with the green bean casserole," Pat said.

"Oh, good," Nancy said. "It should be fine. We should have plenty of food."

She seemed to be fretting more than normal about the amount of food, which made me wonder if there was something else going on. "There's ten of us, right? Did someone not bring something they were supposed to?"

She gave me a weak smile. "Well, about that. Why don't we get inside, and we can talk about it. There's no sense standing out here in the cold." She squinted at the gray sky. "It's not supposed to storm, but I don't know. It's not looking good."

"I guess a first snow for Thanksgiving wouldn't be the worst," Pat said, glancing at me. I could see she had the same trepidation I had about this Thanksgiving dinner.

"No, maybe it would make it even more festive," Nancy said, a forced brightness in her voice as she stepped into the hotel, with us following after. Even though she was carrying more than both of us, she somehow managed to balance it to shut the door behind us.

The warmth of the hotel hit me first, from a huge fire that was roaring in the lobby's giant fireplace, and the woodsy smoky scent filled the room. Overstuffed couches and chairs in a rustic style were clustered around the fireplace, with a bear rug on the floor and handmade quilts hung on the walls. In honor of Thanksgiving, she had decorated the mantel with colorful squashes and dried corn.

"It looks like dessert has arrived." A man holding a glass of wine emerged from the doorway to the right that led to a large, multi-purpose room. In the mornings, it was where Nancy served breakfast and, at other times of the day, it was often used by hotel guests or townspeople for meetings or whatnot.

The man had sandy brown hair, cut short and neat, brown eyes, a round face that was a bit doughy and sporting a perfunctory smile. He was dressed in a brown sweater over a white shirt and jeans that looked pressed, and he had a bit of a paunch. "I'm Tom." He started to offer us a hand and then realized none of us had a free hand to shake.

"This is Charlie and Pat," Nancy said, nodding at each of us. "And Tiki, of course." Tiki wagged her tail politely. "Tom has been staying here at the hotel."

Tom beamed. "And I'm so glad I did. Nancy is a wonderful host, really goes above and beyond, like inviting me to your Thanksgiving get-together. I've been really pleased with my stay."

"We're happy to have you," Nancy said, but was drowned out by loud voices coming from the kitchen.

Pat raised an eyebrow. "I guess Ginny and kids are here."

"About that ..." Nancy started to say, but the voices were getting louder, and a group of people burst out of the kitchen.

"This is what you always do," one of the men was saying, his voice sharp with anger. "You think the world revolves around you, and you can do whatever you want. Well, newsflash, it doesn't."

"It's not my fault your life hasn't turned out the way you wanted it to," a second man said, but unlike the anger in the first man's voice, his sounded more resigned.

"Boys, boys," Ginny said, a pleading note in her voice. "Can't we give it a rest? It's Thanksgiving."

The first man, the angry one, stopped short when he saw us. "Oh, I didn't realize more people had arrived." His mouth worked, as if he was trying to remember how to smile.

"Yes," Nancy said. "This is Charlie and Pat."

"And Tiki," Tom said.

"And Tiki," Nancy agreed. Tiki gave a little, hesitant wag of her tail, as if she wasn't sure about being the center of attention the way she normally was.

"Hi, Tiki," a woman said, stumbling slightly as she stepped forward and almost spilled her wine. "Oh, my goodness, aren't you cute!"

Tiki gave her an uneasy look.

"So, Ginny you know," Nancy said. Ginny fluttered her fingers at us. Even though she was pushing seventy, I had always thought she looked fit and youthful for her age, but not today. Her green eyes had dark circles under them, and her copper-colored hair looked more garish than normal, although maybe that was because it clashed with the orange pumpkins on her light brown sweater. "And these are her children; Miriam, Elias, and Caleb."

Even if Nancy hadn't introduced them, or I hadn't heard them arguing, it was obvious they were related. All three were tall and thin, with similar shades of reddish-brown hair and greenish-brown eyes. Miriam's hair was the most red, while Elias's the most brown and Caleb's was somewhere in the middle.

"Nice to meet you," Caleb said with a wry smile. "I'm sure this is exactly how you wanted to spend Thanksgiving, in the middle of a family squabble."

Elias rolled his eyes. "Oh, give it a rest. Like you care about anyone else's holiday. If you did, you never would have come home."

"Elias," Ginny snapped. "That's your brother you're talking about."

Elias pressed his lips together before taking a long drink of wine.

"And this is Ford," Nancy said, indicating another man standing slightly behind Caleb. He was shorter, with a soft round body and a shock of bright red hair. "Their cousin."

Cousin? I eyed Pat, who looked as confused as I was. "Oh, I didn't realize your cousin was staying at the hotel."

"He's not," Nancy said shortly.

"He decided to tag along with Caleb," Miriam said. "Just like always." Her lips twisted in a sardonic smile as she took a drink.

I looked at Nancy, who gave me a helpless look. "Yes, it appears we have an extra person for dinner."

I turned back to the group in front of me, who were all staring at me in a slightly discomforting way, and made myself smile. "Well, then. I guess it's a good thing I brought four pies. That should be plenty for eleven people."

"Uh," Nancy said. "It's actually twelve."

I gave Nancy a quick look. "Twelve? But I thought …"

"Hi, Charlie," a deep voice said.

I whirled around to see Officer Brandon Wyle walk out of the kitchen with Tilde behind him. "Wyle? I didn't realize you were going to be here."

He shrugged. "Nancy invited me."

"And me, too," Tilde piped in.

I looked back at Nancy, who was looking a little shamefaced. "Uh … I was sure I mentioned it to you."

"You did not," I said through my clenched teeth. Next to me, Pat coughed loudly, but I think that was more to hide the smile on her face.

Officer Brandon Wyle and I were friends and nothing more, even though everyone and their brother seemed to be trying to push us together. I thought Pat was bad, but what Nancy just did was a whole other level. Not telling me that she invited him, no wonder why she kept telling me to bring more pies. Argh.

It didn't help that Wyle was looking awfully good in an emerald green sweater that clung to his broad shoulders and tight jeans. His dark hair, always a little too long, was swept across his shoulder, revealing dark penetrating eyes.

In contrast, Tilde looked more like she was celebrating Easter rather than Thanksgiving. She wore a bright orange sweater with a funky-looking turkey on the front. The color of her sweater clashed with her hair, which was dyed an orange red, and she wore huge, orange-rimmed glasses.

"Glad you brought the pies," Wyle said, coming forward. "Would you like some help with them?"

Nancy started. "Oh, my. Yes, we should get all of this in the kitchen." She made a move toward the kitchen when her head snapped around. "Oh, Doug. There you are. Perfect timing. We're all here now."

I turned to see a man standing on the stairs, an odd expression on his face. He was on the short side, but looked like he worked out regularly—his long-sleeved button down red flannel shirt was straining at the shoulders. His light brown hair was carefully styled, probably to try to minimize the bald spot at the top, and his gray eyes were wary.

"Um … wow. Are you sure there's going to be enough food?" he asked uncertainly. I didn't think there was going to be that many people coming …" His voice trailed off.

"Nonsense," Nancy said cheerfully. Apparently, now that she knew there was enough pie for everyone, she was back to her normal chipper mood. "There's plenty for all of us. Come on down and meet everyone."

After a long pause, so long I was thinking he might turn around and head back to his room, Doug continued down the stairs.

"Doug, let me introduce you to everyone," Nancy said once he was at the bottom of the steps and proceeded to rattle off everyone's name. To his credit, Doug attempted to smile and nod to each person as he was introduced, but by the time she reached Ginny's gang, his expression had frozen into an expression of terror, and I was sure in about two seconds he was going to bolt to his room, never to be seen again.

Tom, however, stepped in to save the day. "Great to officially meet you," he said, holding his hand out to Doug. "I've seen you in the breakfast room every day, but it's nice to now have a name to go with the face."

With some effort, Doug tore his gaze away from Ginny's three kids and looked at Tom. "It's nice to meet you too," he managed, and shook Tom's hand. "Sorry, I'm ..." he swallowed hard. "I've never been good with crowds."

"Then you definitely need to stick with me," Tom said, clapping him on the back. "I live for a good party. I'll be happy to run interference for you."

"I don't like crowds either," Caleb said as Elias rolled his eyes and muttered something under his breath. "I've found a drink helps. Can I get you one?"

"Yes, a drink," Tom said before Doug could answer. "In fact, I think we all need a drink. Or a refill." His eyes lingered on Miriam.

"I agree," Nancy said. "A drink before dinner."

"We can bring it out," I said, shooting Nancy a pointed look. "Since we have food to put away, anyway."

"Yes," Nancy said, finally getting the hint. "Give us a moment to put everything away and we'll be right out with drinks."

"What kind of pies did you make?" Tom asked, before giving me an embarrassed smile. "I have to tell you, ever since Nancy told me you were bringing homemade pies, my mouth has been watering. I can't even remember the last time I had homemade pie for Thanksgiving."

"Pumpkin, pecan, and mincemeat," I said.

Tom's eyes lit up. "Mincemeat? Seriously? I haven't had mincemeat pie since I was a kid. My grandma used to make the most awesome mincemeat pie."

"Mine, too," Ford said. "Oh, man, I've dreamed about her mincemeat pie."

"What are you talking about?" Elias asked. "Grandma never made mincemeat pie."

Ford looked at him like he was an idiot. "My other grandma. The one not related to you."

Elias's cheeks turned red, and he took another long swallow of his wine.

"Give us a minute," I said, plastering a pleasant smile on my face as I moved deliberately toward the kitchen. "We'll be right back with drinks."

"Yes," Nancy said, finally getting the hint as I marched into the kitchen, "we'll be out in a jiffy."

Pat was right on my heels, and she leaned over to whisper into my ear. "Do you think it's too late to take the pies and go home?"

Chapter 4

"How could you?" I hissed to Nancy the moment she entered the kitchen. The air was full of scents of turkey and sage. It was also cleaner than I had would have expected, especially after being used to cook a Thanksgiving meal. Other than a handful of specialized utensils, such as a mortar and pestle, a turkey baster, a few knives, and a garlic press, which were all neatly arranged in a corner next to the large farm sink, the kitchen was spotless.

Nancy looked at me, her expression almost hurt. "I didn't know about Ford, I swear. This was as much of a surprise to me as it was to —"

"I'm not talking about Ford," I said, shoving the dish I was carrying onto the counter and turning to face her, my hands on my hips. "I'm talking about Wyle. He didn't just 'show up.'" I flapped my hands. "You knew and didn't tell me."

Nancy's eyes widened slightly, and she gave me an innocent look. "Oh. Are you sure? I really thought I had mentioned it."

"Don't give me that. You didn't mention it. I went through all the names this morning and —" I broke off as Wyle pushed open the kitchen door, holding one of the pies.

"Where can I put it?" he asked, balancing it on one hand.

"Oh, you can put it right there," Nancy said, pointing to where I was standing. "Thanks for your help. I better get out there; we've got thirsty guests." She winked at me as she picked up a wine bottle and a platter full of cheese, sausage, and crackers, and headed out the door.

Pat was shoving her salad into the oversized fridge. "Don't mind me," she said. "As soon as I get this in here, I'll go help Nancy."

"You don't have to leave," I said, just as Pat slammed the fridge shut, and reached for another bottle of wine and a couple of glasses.

"I don't mind helping Nancy," Pat said, flashing me a small mischievous smile before backing out of the kitchen. Even Tiki seemed to be in on it, giving me a quick tail wag before disappearing with Pat out of the door.

I closed my eyes. I should have just stayed home.

"So, where do you want the pie?" Wyle asked, and my eyes flew open. He was standing in front of me, a bemused expression on his face.

I put my hands on my hips. "You could have told me you were coming here for Thanksgiving."

He shrugged. "I don't remember discussing our Thanksgiving plans. And I could say the same about you."

"But you must have known I was going to be here," I said. "I'm sure Nancy said something, especially since I've been coming here for years. This is your first time. Why would you mention something?" My eyes narrowed as my words sunk in. "Wait a minute. Why *are* you here? Why aren't you where you normally go for Thanksgiving?"

"I'm working tomorrow, so it didn't make sense to drive the three hours to visit my parents, which is what I normally do."

"But how did Nancy find out?"

"Because I told her. We're having a torrid affair, you know."

He said *what*? I felt like one of those cartoon characters where my eyes bugged out of my sockets.

Wyle took one look at my face and burst out laughing. "You should see yourself. Honestly, Charlie, what are you, Nancy's keeper or something? Why do you care?"

"I was just curious is all," I muttered, wishing the floor would open up and swallow me. This dinner was turning into a massive disaster. I was starting to think Pat's husband, home with food poisoning, was the lucky one.

Wyle took a step closer to me, close enough I could smell the scent of his shampoo and soap on his skin. "If you must know, Nancy had overheard me talk about not visiting my parents when I was having lunch at Aunt May's, and she invited me to come over. So I accepted."

Now I was starting to feel a little foolish. "Oh, I guess that makes sense." He was too close to me. I wanted to move away from him, but he was also effectively blocking my way to the door. "I should probably leave and go help Nancy and Pat," I said, gesturing feebly with my hands, as if that would get him to move.

It didn't. He stayed where he was, studying me, his head cocked. "You know, it's not like I was trying to hide anything from you. I asked you a number of times to have lunch or dinner with me. As a friend." He shot me a meaningful look. "You were the one who kept telling me how busy you were."

"Well, my business is growing, so you know." I flapped my hands uselessly again.

It was true he had been asking me to join him for a meal, and it was also true I had been avoiding him. Despite his reassurances that we would only be spending time as friends, I knew deep down if we started seeing each other, that would change.

And there was no way I could date anyone, much less a cop. Not with my history.

Wyle looked like he was going to say something, but at that moment Nancy poked her head in. "Sorry, I'm not trying to disturb you two, but I forgot the napkins and the little plates. Can you bring them?"

"Of course," I said, ducking past Wyle and grabbing what Nancy had asked for. The plates were her normal small ones she put out when serving cookies and whatnot, white with a little gold rim. The paper napkins, however, were Thanksgiving themed with an overflowing cornucopia on them.

"I guess we should join the party," I said, heading toward the door.

Wyle shot me a look. "You know we're not done with this conversation yet."

"Of course not," I said, moving toward the door. "It wouldn't be Thanksgiving without uncomfortable conversations." *And this one is going to have more than its share*, I mentally added as I stepped into the lobby.

Nancy spotted me and waved me over, although it wasn't like I couldn't see that everyone had gathered around the fireplace. Tiki was weaving through the crowd, alternating between getting pets and treats from people and licking the crumbs off the polished wooden floor.

"She's been the vacuum cleaner," Nancy was saying as I joined them.

"What, no drink?" Tom said, as I arranged the napkins and plates on the little wooden coffee table. "Let me remedy that immediately. Wine?"

"Sure," I said. Tom moved to a table in the corner of the room that had been turned into a makeshift bar as I headed over to join Pat on the loveseat. Wyle was by the fireplace, poking at the fire.

"Tom was telling us about how he's a traveling medical consultant," Pat said.

"Sort of," Tom said, pouring red wine into an elegant gold and white glass. "I help hospitals and clinics manage their internal radiology departments more effectively or, like in the case of the Redemption hospital, I help them expand their departments."

"And trust me, Redemption desperately needs an upgrade," Tilde said. "Some of the equipment is older than I am."

"I might be a little biased but, yes, I agree, Redemption definitely needs some new equipment," Tom said.

"And not just the radiology department," Tilde said. "The whole hospital needs to be renovated. It's disgraceful." She clucked her tongue as she shook her head.

"Well, uh, I'm glad it's getting done then," I said as I accepted the wine, and wondered if I should tell Pat if anything happened to me, she should make sure I was taken to one of the hospitals in Riverview. "I thought I read something about an expansion, but I didn't realize it was the radiology department."

"Yes, they got a grant, so they're getting all new equipment," Tom said. "It's quite exciting to see it all come together." His cheeks were flushed, although it might be more from the wine than the thought of all that new equipment to play with at the hospital.

"So, you're here only temporarily?" I asked.

Tom nodded as he pulled up one of the armchairs closer to the fire. "My contract is for three months. Normally I would be staying in an apartment, but there was an issue with it."

"A water pipe burst," Nancy said.

"Oh, I guess that would be a problem," I said.

Tom nodded as he took a sip. "It was a real mess, and with the holidays coming up, there was no other short-term rentals immediately available, and who knows how long it's going to take to make that apartment livable, so until then, I'm back here." He grinned at Nancy, who beamed back at him.

I glanced between them, wondering if there was something else going on, although Nancy was quite a bit older than he was. But, hey, if two consensual adults wanted to have a little fun, it was certainly none of my business.

"What about you?" Pat asked Doug, who was hovering in the corner, just outside of the circle of furniture. He was perched on one of the straight-backed chairs and looked extremely uncomfortable.

"Oh, I'm also here for work." He was balancing a glass of wine on one knee and on the other he had a couple of pieces of cheese on a plate. "I'm only here for a few weeks, not like Tom."

"What do you do?" I asked.

He took a swallow of wine. "I work for a big treatment center."

"Treatment center?" Pat asked.

"Treatment for drug and alcohol addiction." He gave his glass of wine a rueful glance. "We're currently expanding and opening up a new center here in Redemption."

"Perfect timing," Miriam said, swirling her wine around in her glass. She had kicked off her expensive-looking high-heeled shoes and was curled up in one of the armchairs that had been pulled closer to the fire. "We can all check ourselves in after this weekend."

"Well, it won't be open quite yet," Doug said with a small smile. "The grand opening isn't until next year."

"Can we book in advance?" Miriam asked, eyeing her brothers. "And can we get a family rate?"

"Speak for yourself, Miriam," Elias said, as he got up to fetch the bottle. "Just because you can't hold your liquor doesn't mean the rest of us can't."

"Oh, I can hold it just fine," she said, holding out her glass and raising her eyebrows meaningfully. "Just as good as you, dear brother. Which seems to me *is* the definition of needing an alcohol treatment center, don't you think?"

"It's nice seeing you again, Miriam," Pat said, before Elias could argue with her, although I noticed he came over to refill his sister's glass. "We haven't seen you back here very much in recent years."

"She travels a lot," Ginny said. "For her job."

"A little too much," Miriam said, her eyes on Elias as he filled her glass. "I was supposed to be in Europe right now."

"Europe," Pat said. "That's exciting. I would love to visit Europe."

Miriam let out a noise that was probably supposed to be a laugh, but it sounded more like a yelp. "It's not that exciting I assure you, at least if you're there for business. It's exhausting trying to attend meetings while you're fighting jet lag. By the time you've adjusted to the time zone, you have to fly back."

"I can imagine that would be difficult," I said. "So, what do you do?"

"I'm a VP for an international company," she said, sipping her wine.

"That sounds exciting," I said. That certainly explained the stylish shoes, as well as the designer black and white pantsuit she was wearing.

"Not really," she said. "A lot of paperwork, a lot of meetings. A lot of traveling."

"Oh, don't listen to her," Elias said, rolling his eyes. "She loves telling us how important her job is, don't you, sis?"

"Oh, I can't possibly compete with how important *your* job is," Miriam said, her voice like ice. "You could screw up your company's books, and then where would we be?"

"As I've already told you, I'm an accountant, not a bookkeeper," Elias snapped.

Miriam pressed a hand to her chest. "Oh. My mistake."

Elias glared at her over his wineglass as he took a drink. There was an awkward silence.

"What about you?" Pat asked, looking at Caleb. I know she had been dying to grill Caleb, but she was waiting for the right time. "What do you do?"

He shifted a little uncomfortably in his seat. "I'm in real estate." He and Ford were sitting on the couch, although they were both at opposite ends.

"What, like a realtor?" Pat asked.

"More like real estate investing," he said. His eyes were darker than his siblings', although maybe they just seemed darker because they were certainly more intense. His face was thin and angular, with high, sharp cheekbones, and a broodiness that reminded me of bad boys in romance novels.

"So, you're a landlord, or do you flip houses or something else?" I asked.

"Yes," Caleb said, "all of the above. I have a few different types of real estate investing businesses I'm a part of."

"Any of them legal?" Elias asked.

"Elias, enough already," Ginny said with a long sigh.

"Ford, what about you?" Nancy asked. "What do you do?"

"Oh, this and that," Ford said. He smiled, but it didn't quite reach his eyes. "I'm between things right now."

Ginny's eyes went wide. "Still?" She glanced around the room, as if remembering she wasn't at home, and quickly rearranged her expression. "Sorry. I just … I guess I thought by now, Ford, you'd have figured out what you do with your life." She smiled awkwardly, like she was trying to take the sting out of her words.

Ford, however, didn't seem that concerned. "Don't worry, Aunt Ginny, I've got some prospects I've been working on, and I'm sure something is going to pop."

"I hope so," Ginny said. "You're way too smart and talented to not have a good career."

"Aww, thanks. I can always count on you," Ford said, his smile looking more natural. He picked up the wine bottle and brought it to her, topping off her glass as he leaned down to give her a kiss on the cheek. She giggled like a schoolgirl and swatted his arm. "Oh, you. Always such a charmer."

I noticed his cousins didn't seem to be nearly as taken with Ford as their mother was. All three of them were looking anywhere but at their mother.

"So, Charlie, is it?" Tom asked, filling a small plate with cheese and crackers, seemingly oblivious to the tension in the room. "Did I hear correctly that you're a professional baker? I have to tell you, I have been waiting all week to taste your pies."

"Actually, I make custom teas and tinctures," I said.

Tom's eyebrows went up. "Oh? I'm sure Nancy said you were a professional baker, and some of the cookies and muffins came from you."

"No, no, no, not the baked goods," Nancy said. "I bake all of those myself. The herbal teas are from Charlie. Like the lemon lavender one."

"Oh, that's a really good one," Tom said, looking a little more impressed. "You made that?"

"Yes. I grow many of the herbs and flowers in my backyard as well, and then I turn them into teas," I said. "Not the lemon, obviously, but the lavender is from my garden."

"Wow. I didn't even know that was even possible," Tom said. "So, you sell them as well? Like, do you have a store somewhere?"

"No store. I just sell them out of my home," I said, "either directly to clients or to other businesses like Nancy."

"Huh. I never would have thought of having a business like that," Tom said.

"Does that mean the pies are going to be a disappointment?" Ford asked.

"Are you kidding?" Pat said. "As good as her teas are, her baking is just as good. Trust me, if Charlie had wanted a business selling pies and cookies, she'd have one."

"She's a wonderful baker," Nancy said. "I never would have asked her to make the pies if I didn't think she could handle it."

"Well, that's a relief," Tom said. "After looking forward to her pies all week, I would hate it if it was a disappointment."

"I agree," Ford said. "Especially since now that I know there's going to be mincemeat."

Tom rubbed his stomach. "No kidding."

"Hey," Wyle said. He had been so quiet I had almost forgotten he was there. Well, maybe I should say, him being quiet was making it easier for me to forget he was there. "Did you see how dark it's gotten outside? I think it might be storming."

We all craned our heads toward the front windows, but it was impossible to see what was happening with the weather, as it was pitch black outside.

"How can you tell it's storming?" Pat asked. "I can't see a thing out there."

"Neither can I," Nancy said. She had gotten up and had joined Wyle, who was walking toward the door.

"I can't tell if it's snowing or … is it sleeting?" Wyle asked.

"It could be freezing rain," Pat said, getting to her feet.

"Oh, I hope it's not freezing rain," Nancy said. "We could be in for another ice storm."

"That would be bad," Pat said. "Remember the last one we had back in the seventies? We didn't have power for three days."

"Three days," Tom said. "You didn't have any electricity in the middle of winter for three days?"

"It was scary," Pat said.

"That reminds me," Nancy said. "In case we lose power, I should check …"

Before she could finish her sentence, the lights went out.

Chapter 5

"No one panic," Wyle said even though, from how it sounded, everyone was panicking. And talking. And a scream or two. I thought it was probably Miriam, but it was possible it was Ginny. Or maybe Nancy. It was hard to tell with the room completely dark, other than the light from the fireplace which, rather than helping matters, seemed to add to the shadows and confusion.

There was a loud thud, the sounds of someone swearing, and then an angry-sounding yip, which made me wonder if Tiki had gotten stepped on.

"I've got candles and flashlights, just let me get … ouch. Drat," Nancy muttered as something loud clattered on the floor.

"Everyone stop panicking," Tilde yelled.

"You stepped on me," Miriam shrieked.

"Ouch … crap … I can't see anything," another voice responded, which sounded like Tom.

"Tiki, where are you?" Pat called out, crouching down.

"Everyone, just take a breath," Wyle said, his voice calm and authoritative. "We all need to stay where we are until Nancy can locate candles and flashlights."

"Yes," Tilde said. "Where are the candles and flashlights, Nancy? I can help find them … ouch." Another crash, this one sounded like one of the chairs getting knocked over. "Drat, that hurt."

"What we really need is more wine," Elias said.

"Oh, there you are," Pat said, her voice relieved as she stood up next to me. I could just make out enough to see her holding the wiggly body of Tiki, who was busy giving her kisses on her nose. "Yes, you're a good girl."

"Nancy, where are your candles and flashlights?" Ginny asked.

"They're right … ow," Nancy said.

"Hold on," Wyle said. "Let me help."

It was still somewhat chaotic, and it seemed everyone had knocked or bumped into something, but eventually Nancy located about a half dozen flashlights and passed them out, which meant we had to share. Because Pat was holding Tiki, I was given one for both of us, although it was more like a pen light than a real flashlight, but at least it was something.

Candles, however, were another story. Nancy had brought out at least two dozen along with a bunch of holders, and had gone back for more, but Wyle told her that was probably enough. We didn't want to burn down the hotel after all. Once we had them placed and lit on every available surface, they ended up illuminating the lobby with a soft, orange glow.

"Everyone okay?" Wyle asked. He was slowly prowling around the lobby with his flashlight pointed toward the ground, casting him in shadow. It was almost like he had ceased to be human and had turned into a silhouette, flitting around the room.

Or maybe a ghost.

I shivered, folding my arms across my chest but being careful not to point my tiny flashlight in anyone's face.

"We will be," Tom said, holding a bottle of wine in one hand and his flashlight in the other. The bottle cast a long shadow across the floor. "Any takers?"

"Oh, thank goodness," Miriam said, holding up her glass. "Yes, please."

"I think we can all use a refill," Elias said as Tom topped off Miriam's glass.

"That's for sure," Ford said, holding out his own for Tom.

"How bad is it out there?" Ginny asked, a nervous twitch in her voice. "Are we looking at another ice storm?"

"It's bad," Wyle said grimly. "Definitely freezing rain coming down, but whether it's going to become another ice storm is yet to be determined. I'll call it in and see what I can find out. Nancy, can I use your phone?"

"Go ahead. It's on the check-in desk," Nancy said, adjusting a candle in the holder to make it straighter. "I've got some kerosene lamps in the basement. Should I dig them out?"

"Not yet," I said. "I think the candles and flashlights are fine for now."

"What about dinner?" Tom asked. "Does this mean no turkey?"

"I have a gas stove," Nancy said. "Besides, everything is pretty much done. I'll check it in a minute. That was fast. What did they say?" she said to Wyle, who had returned to the group.

"There's no dial tone," Wyle said.

"No phones or electricity?" Tom asked. "I guess the weather must be bad."

"Or maybe it's our resident ghost playing a trick on us," Nancy said.

"Of course, there's a ghost in the hotel," Elias said. "It wouldn't be Redemption if there wasn't a ghost involved somehow."

"You didn't say anything about a ghost when I checked in," Doug said. His tone was forced, like he was trying to make a joke, but underneath I could hear the stress.

"I assure you she's harmless," Nancy said. "Although she can be a bit of a trickster. Turning off all the lights and phone on Thanksgiving is definitely up her alley, especially since there are several men here." She winked.

"Why men?" Tilde asked.

"Darla tends to only show herself to men," Nancy said. "Probably because of what happened to her."

"Wait," Doug said. "You have a ghost that only shows herself to men, and you didn't think to tell me?"

"Honestly, you have nothing to worry about," Nancy said. "She's only killed someone one time. Well, maybe twice."

Doug's eyes went wide. "She's killed people?"

"It was an accident," Nancy said. "Darla doesn't mean to hurt anyone. She's usually very friendly."

"Friendly?" Doug asked, his voice growing louder. "You're trying to tell me we have a homicidal ghost in this hotel that targets men?"

"Honestly, you're blowing this out of proportion," Nancy said.

"Why doesn't she like men?" Tilde asked.

"Well, it probably has to do with how she became a ghost," Nancy said. "According to local legend, it was the summer before the stock market crashed, back in 1929. She and her husband were visiting. My understanding is they were newlyweds, but I'm not sure when they were married. Darla suffered from terrible headaches and would take laudanum for them. One night, her husband went out for cigarettes and never came back. Darla was so distraught she took all her laudanum and ended overdosing and dying."

"Ah, the old going-out-for-cigarettes excuse," Tilde said. "No wonder why she hates men."

"I didn't say she hated men," Nancy corrected. "She only shows herself to men. It could be she's flirting with them. It's hard to tell with a ghost."

"Yes, it's definitely difficult to figure out if a ghost is flirting with you or trying to kill you," Pat said drily.

"Well, when you've been a ghost for so long, it's easy to forget what it was like when you were human," Nancy explained.

"How does she show herself?" Tilde asked. "Do they actually see her?"

"Some men have reported seeing something like an apparition," Nancy said. "There's also strange sounds and cold spots. You know, the usual types of things that show up in a haunting."

"So, how is she killing people?" Tilde asked.

"I think she's just scaring them to death, but I'm sure she doesn't mean to," Nancy said. "They have a heart attack or get startled and fall down the stairs. That sort of thing."

"Somehow, that doesn't make me feel any better," Doug said.

"I kind of agree," Tilde said. "Maybe it would be worthwhile to find a way to get her to leave? Maybe find out what happened to her husband all those years ago, and that might give her some closure."

"This is Redemption," Pat said. "Any ghosts that show up are here to stay."

"Why is that?" Tom asked.

"Because the town is cursed," Caleb said.

"Wait. Did you say cursed?" Tom asked.

"Yes, Redemption is cursed," Caleb said flatly.

"I wouldn't go that far," Nancy said quickly. "It does have a rather troubling past, but I wouldn't call it cursed."

"Redemption has a troubling past?" Tom asked, taking a step backwards.

"Maybe troubling is too strong of a word," Nancy said.

"Well, I don't know, how else would you describe adults disappearing?" Tilde asked.

"People disappear in this town?" Tom asked.

"Not recently," Nancy said.

"Yeah, I think the last big disappearance was three or four years ago," Tilde said.

Tom's head was swiveling around as if he was trying to look at all of us at once. "You're kidding, right? This is all a big joke."

"It's not as bad as they're making it seem," Wyle said. "Yes, Redemption does have a history of people disappearing, but people disappear from all towns. It's not that unusual."

"Didn't anyone tell you the history of the town?" Pat asked.

"Not really," Tom said. "I guess I heard a few things, but I dismissed them as an old wives' tale, so I didn't pay much attention."

"It's not an old wives' tale," Tilde said. "It really happened."

"What really happened?" Tom asked.

"All the adults disappearing," Tilde said.

Tom gave his head a quick shake. "That actually happened? Why wasn't it in the national news?"

"Because it wasn't recent," Pat said. "It was back in 1888."

"It was a terrible winter," Nancy said. "Horrible blizzards. There was one in particular called the Children's Blizzard. Did you hear about it? No, well, it doesn't matter. At one point during that terrible winter, all the adults disappeared."

"From what people wrote about the children's' story, when they went to bed their parents were there, and when they woke up they were gone," Tilde said.

"Seriously?" While I couldn't see him very well, it sure sounded like Tom's jaw had dropped. "What happened to them?"

"No one knows," Tilde said.

"Still?"

"There's a lot of rumors and stories, but no, no one knows what happened to the adults," Nancy said.

"That was just the start," Caleb said. "This town has a long history of strange and unexplained events. Now do you see why Redemption is cursed?"

"I would say so," Tom said.

"It's not cursed," Nancy said again. "Most of the people who visit or live here are perfectly fine."

"Somehow that's not very comforting," Tom said. "Especially when there's no light or phone, and a storm is raging outside."

"Caleb, if you believe this town is cursed, then why did you bother coming back?" Elias said.

Caleb seemed to shrink into himself. "I told you. My plans changed, and I thought it would be nice to see family."

Elias snorted. "I was talking about the real reason."

"Of course, that's the real reason," Ginny said. "Why wouldn't Caleb want to see family? That's why you're here, right? To spend time with your family."

"I'm here because my wife refused to let me see my family," Elias said tightly, but almost immediately realized what he had said. "I didn't mean that. I just meant ..."

"I know," Ginny said quietly. "You miss your kids. Trust me, I understand. More than you know."

There was an awkward silence, then Ginny pulled her shawl around her tighter. "So, there's no phone or electricity. Does this mean the heat is going to shut off, too?"

"The heat will be fine," Nancy said, her voice relieved at the change of subject. "It's gas, too, but even if there is a problem, I have plenty of wood and we can keep the fire burning all night. If the weather is too bad for everyone to leave, I've got enough cots and beds for everyone to spend the night. We'll be fine."

"Just like we were kids and had a big sleepover," Miriam said, and half-turned toward her brothers. "Although this time, Debbie isn't here." Her tone was pointed.

"Oh, Debbie," Ginny said. "I hadn't thought about her in ages. Such a sweet girl."

"Yes, very sweet," Miriam said, a bite to her voice. "That's probably what the attraction was, isn't that right?"

"Oh, stop it, Miriam," Elias said, his voice bitter. "Why do you have to bring up ancient history now? No one wants to hear about this."

"What ancient history?" Ginny asked. "Did one of your brothers have a little crush on Debbie?"

"I wouldn't call it having a little crush," Miriam said. "More like stalking."

"Miriam," Ginny gasped. "How could you say that about Elias?"

"Me?" Elias nearly spit out his wine. "Why do you assume it was me she was talking about and not Caleb?"

"Because you and Miriam were always fighting," Ginny said. "Caleb was the peacemaker."

"Caleb was hardly the peacemaker," Elias said. "He was playing you. You never saw it ..."

"Elias, stop it." Ginny put her hands over her ears. "Isn't this stressful enough without you starting an argument? Besides, it's

Thanksgiving, and it's the first time we've been together as a family for years. Can't we just enjoy it?"

"*Enjoy* it?" Elias's voice went up a notch. "You want us to pretend to be one big happy family when one of your children is probably a psychopath."

"Elias," Ginny snapped. "I said *enough*."

"You just refuse to see the truth about him," Elias said. "What he did —"

"We should eat," Nancy interrupted, her voice unnaturally bright as she quickly stood up. "Does anyone want to help me with the food?"

"I will," I said, just as quickly, standing up.

"Me, too," Pat said.

"I also need some help finishing setting the table and moving all of these candles to the breakfast room, if anyone wants to come," Nancy said as she headed to the kitchen, a flashlight in one hand and another one holding a candle. "I figured it would make the most sense to eat in there, as that's already set up for when we eat in the mornings. Don't you agree?" She didn't pause for an answer, and instead just kept a steady stream of chatter, maybe she didn't want to give Elias a chance to start the argument again.

Everyone other than Elias, who was muttering darkly into his drink, jumped to their feet and started picking up candles to carefully carry them into the breakfast room. "I have more candles as well, if that's not enough," Nancy called out as she kicked open the door.

"I'm sure we have plenty of candles," Wyle said from somewhere behind us.

I wasn't expecting the kitchen to be as dark as it was. Nancy tucked the candle on a side counter next to the flashlight that she left on and went immediately to the oven to open it. Pat put Tiki on the ground and we both went to help Nancy dish up the turkey and all the side dishes. Outside the door, I could hear the sounds of bickering but I couldn't hear what was specifically being said.

"Oh, dear," Nancy said, lifting the turkey out of the oven and putting it on the counter. "This isn't going very well."

"You think?" Pat asked, grabbing an oven mitt to pull out the sides.

"Maybe I should have told Ginny not to come," Nancy said, rummaging around in a drawer before finally pulling out an electric carving knife.

"I don't think that's going to work," I said, as Nancy started unwinding the cord.

"Oh." She stared at it, bewildered. "You're right. What am I thinking? I'm so discombobulated and I'm going to have to carve this by hand?"

"I can do it," Pat said, rolling up her sleeves. "I've carved plenty a turkey by hand in my day."

Nancy didn't move, but just stared at the turkey. "I didn't feel right telling her not to come, but I had a feeling it wasn't going to end well. All that bad blood."

I put a hand on her arm. "Hey, you couldn't know. I would have still invited them. After all, they're all adults. Wouldn't you think they could control themselves for one day?"

"Besides, it's Thanksgiving," Pat said, checking out the wooden knife block to see what sort of knives she had at her disposal. "Thanksgiving is all about eating too much, drinking too much, and arguing with your family. Usually about politics, but also past hurts and disappointments and misunderstandings work, too."

A small smile touched Nancy's lips. "True."

I started looking for serving dishes for the mashed potatoes and stuffing. "Do you really think that's the reason why Caleb decided to come home now? Because his plans changed?"

"I don't know." Nancy moved away from the turkey so Pat could start to carve and toward the fridge. "That is what Ginny told me, that his original plans had been canceled, and it was a last-minute decision. But, I also didn't have a chance to talk with her in private."

"Seems a little suspicious," Pat said as the kitchen door opened and Tilde appeared.

"What's suspicious?" Tilde asked.

"Why the lights and the phone went out the way they did," Pat said. Pat wasn't a huge fan of Tilde's amateur sleuthing, because she thought Tilde was just as likely to mess something up as she was to solve a crime. It made her sound a little like Wyle and why he didn't want us getting involved in police work. Although, to be fair, he was also constantly telling me how dangerous it was and how I was opening myself up to getting hurt. "I know there's a storm out," Pat continued, an odd note in her tone, "but it still feels like something else is going on. Something bigger."

I opened my mouth to respond, then closed it. Now that Pat said it, I could see what she was talking about. It did feel like there was something else going on, something more than just a fluke ice storm over Thanksgiving. There was a reason why we were all brought together this evening, and it wasn't a good one.

"Well, what do you expect?" Tilde asked. "It is Redemption."

Chapter 6

"Thank you again for inviting me to join you," Tom said, helping himself to mashed potatoes. "I can't even remember the last time I had a home cooked meal for Thanksgiving."

"Thanksgiving is all about friends and family," Nancy said, arranging the stuffing and gravy in front of him. Tom was taking his own sweet time filling his plate, which meant there were now a number of dishes piled up next to him.

Not that it mattered. There was no rush. The electricity was still out, but just as Nancy had promised, the heat was still on and the room was toasty warm. The air was filled with the savory smells of food, and the lit candles contributed a festive glow, making it feel like the lack of electric light was a purposeful choice.

"It truly is," Tom said, a pensive look on his face. "Unfortunately, with my travel schedule, I'm not able to spend holidays with friends or family. Not that I have much family left." He smiled as he said it, but it was strained.

"I know the feeling," I said, my thoughts straying to my own sad family situation. "I'm just grateful I have such good friends." I leaned closer to Pat to bump her shoulder, and she smiled at me.

"I agree, friends are important too," Tom said, the pensive look still on his face. "And unfortunately for me, my travel schedule also has wreaked havoc on that front, too." He paused, still holding the spoon for the mashed potatoes in the air. "I love my job. I really do. The excitement of going to a new place and building something from scratch." He looked around the table, his cheeks flushed with either wine or passion. "And the best part is what we build is making a huge difference in the local communities. We're literally helping save lives." He paused again, the excitement dimming in his face. "But I would be lying if I said there wasn't a cost. At least personally."

"Yeah, that's a tough one," I said. "It's hard to make a decision between your life's work and friends and family."

He nodded, then looked at the mashed potato spoon he still held in his hand, like he had forgotten about it, before putting it back and moving on to the gravy.

"So, you never married?" Tilde asked. I winced inwardly. Tilde was always one to wade right in, no matter how personal the question was.

"Actually, I was married." He gave Tilde a faint smile. "Divorced."

"Oh," Tilde said. "I'm sorry to hear that."

He waved a hand, although it was unfortunately the one holding the gravy spoon, and splatters of the brown gravy fell in a fine mist on the white tablecloth. "It's fine. It was amicable. She couldn't handle all the moving around. She wanted to find a place and settle in. But …" he shrugged, "that wasn't in the cards."

"Well," Nancy said, nudging the stuffing closer, likely in hopes he would get the hint. "I'm glad you were here this Thanksgiving, so you could be part of a proper celebration."

"Me, too," Tom said, plopping the spoon in the gravy boat so forcefully some of it spilled over, and then reached for the stuffing.

"What about you?" Tilde asked, turning her head toward Doug. "What's a typical Thanksgiving celebration for you?"

Doug had just put a bite of turkey in his mouth, but he froze, mid-chew. "Um … I don't really have a lot of friends or family, either."

"Well, we're glad you could join us," Nancy said firmly, shooting Tilde a look.

Tilde didn't take the hint. "That's too bad. It must be rough during the holidays for you."

Doug took a moment to chew and swallow his food. "It's not as bad as you might think. I'm a loner, so I like my alone time, plus this time of year is always really busy for me. My job requires me to do a lot of schmoozing, so I'm attending a lot of holiday parties. It's actually kind of a relief to spend the actual holiday alone." A faint smile touched his lips.

I glanced down at my food, mostly to hide my expression, as I was having a hard time believing this shy man had a job that required him to schmooze.

Tilde seemed to be thinking the same thing. "That's nice. You're able to enjoy holiday parties now, even if you're spending the actual holiday alone. What were holidays like when you were growing up?"

"Probably exactly like this one," Elias said, reaching for his wine. "Some great-aunt he only saw twice a year giving him the third degree."

"Elias," Ginny said. "There's no need to be rude."

"What?" Elias said, swirling his wine. "I'm just pointing out what's happening." He flashed Tilde a meaningful look.

Tilde looked a little hurt. "I'm just making conversation. We haven't gotten to know Doug at all yet, and I thought it would be nice to."

"Maybe he doesn't want to share," Elias said. "Did you think about that?"

"Maybe he *does* want to share and hasn't been able to get a word in edge-wise because you and your family have been so obnoxious," Tilde said tartly. "Have you thought about that?"

Miriam burst out laughing and even Caleb hid a smile behind his wineglass. "She's got your number," Miriam said.

Elias didn't look amused. "Not everyone wants to share all their deep, dark secrets."

"What deep dark secrets?" Tilde asked. "I was just asking about his family. If he doesn't want to share, he doesn't have to."

"It's fine," Doug said. "I've never been great about talking about myself. It's not something I've ever been comfortable doing."

"I hear you," Ford said. "I've never liked talking about myself, either." Miriam rolled her eyes at that but didn't say anything.

"But, to answer your question, there's really nothing to say. Growing up, everything was pretty normal, like you would expect with any other family, and that included how we celebrated holidays," Doug said.

"Well, it's nice you have those memories," Tilde said. "I always think it's good for children to grow up celebrating holidays with their family. Very healthy."

"Just as long as you aren't spending those holidays listening to your family argue," Elias said.

"Not everyone's family argues during the holidays," Tilde said.

"Oh, I would say most do," Elias said.

"Elias, I don't know what has gotten into you," Ginny said. "Our family never fought during the holidays. Why would you say such a thing?"

"If that was the case," Elias said, spreading his hands out. "Why has it been years since we spent a holiday together as a family? You'd think if we had such wonderful memories, we'd be spending every holiday together."

Ginny's jaw dropped. "Well, it's difficult." She was stuttering on her words. "You had your family to spend time with, and Miriam was traveling so much, and Caleb was busy. It had nothing to do with what happened when you were children. Heavens, Elias, I don't know where you get these ideas."

Elias's mouth had flattened into a thin line. "Well, all I can say is people who have happy memories of their childhood are probably more likely to spend time with their families when they're an adult. Am I right?" He gave everyone a hard look, and I lowered my head. He wasn't wrong, at least with my family and my strained relationship with my sister, that I still wasn't sure how I could fix.

"I don't think that's always true," Doug said. I jerked my head up to look at him in surprise. "It's not for me. We always got along and had a nice time during the holidays."

"Then why don't you see them anymore?" Elias asked.

"It's not because of anything that happened during the holidays," Doug said. "Family relationships are more complicated than that. And, at least in my case, part of what happened was my fault. I wasn't the easiest child. I had a lot of problems. My poor mother was beside herself. She had no idea how to help me. I know how much she loved me and wanted to protect me. Heck, she would have wrapped me in bubble wrap if she could have." A faraway look was in his eyes and the faint smile was back. "But, unfortunately, you can't protect someone from life. Eventually, they're going to have to grow up and deal with the hand life dealt them. And, in the case of me and my family, unfortunately my family didn't approve of my choices, so it just became easier to not see them." He shrugged and played with a piece of turkey.

There was an awkward pause. "I'm sure you did the best you could at the time," Nancy said, her voice gentle.

Doug gave her a lopsided smile. "I'd like to think so. It's easy to second-guess yourself when looking back on things. But, if there's one thing I've learned while working in addiction recovery, it's the past is the past. You can't change what happened, no matter how much you may want to. All you have is the present."

"Well said," Pat said. Tiki sat up and wagged her tail.

I picked up my wineglass. "To living in the present."

Doug's cheeks flushed pink with pleased embarrassment as everyone else picked up their glass and held it up. "To living in the present."

As I took a sip, I noticed neither Miriam nor Elias looked like they agreed with the toast. Elias, in particular had a sour look on his face as he eyed his brother. Caleb, for his part, took a long, satisfying drink.

If I had hoped the toast might smooth things over, at least for a couple of hours while we finished dinner, I had a feeling I was very much mistaken.

Chapter 7

"What a wonderful meal," Ford said, pushing back his plate with a sigh. "You all outdid yourself."

"I agree," Tom said. "I'm not sure I could eat another bite."

"Of course you can," Ford said with a wink. "There's pie. And as you know, there's always room for pie." Both men chuckled.

Despite the earlier tensions, the rest of dinner had been surprisingly pleasant, which made me wonder, despite my earlier misgivings, if my toast might have helped after all. The conversation was light-hearted, with most people sharing funny work stories. Even Doug had opened up some more, sharing a couple of stories of his own. Tom and Ford especially had hit it off, and both of them had insisted on going back and forth to the kitchen or dining room to fetch more wine or food. "You did more than enough," Tom said, as Nancy tried to protest that they were her guests and should relax. "This is the least we can do."

"We have to do something to earn our keep," Ford said. "Especially if we want to be invited back next year."

Ginny laughed, but her children didn't look amused.

"You should help, too," Ford had said to Caleb at one point, punching him lightly on the shoulder.

"You look like you got it covered for now," Caleb said, but he kept his gaze on his plate.

"It's Thanksgiving. There's always more to do," Ford said.

Caleb glanced up at that and gave him a thin smile. "I'll wait until it's time to clean up. No one likes cleaning things up, right?"

The two men stared at each other. Something seemed to pass between them, but then Ford gave his head a quick shake and shot Caleb a tight-lipped smile. "You're right. You should be the one helping with the cleanup."

"Fat chance," Elias muttered. "You've never helped clean up anything in your life."

Caleb sat back in his chair and eyed his brother. "You have no idea what you're talking about."

"Now, now," Ginny said. "I'm sure you both remember how much I had to harass both of you to do your chores, and the things you would say or do to get out of it. I remember how creative you could both be."

"Yes. My daughter was the same way," Pat said, and then launched into a story, and the tension that had started rising again dissipated.

"I agree," Tilde said. "The meal was wonderful. Best Thanksgiving yet."

"Yes," Doug said. "Thank you again for inviting me." He looked so relaxed it was almost like he had turned into a different person. Or maybe it was the couple of glasses of wine he had drank. His cheeks had turned a rosy pink in the candlelight. "It's been … nice. I guess it's been so long since I had Thanksgiving with my family, I had forgotten how nice it could be spending it with a group."

"Families can be difficult," Tilde said. "It's especially sad when you used to get along and you had a falling out. Do you think there's a chance of a reconciliation?"

"You don't have to talk about it if you don't want to," I said, noticing how Doug seemed to be shrinking in his seat.

"But if it would help to talk about it, we're here," Tilde said. I had to hand it to her, she certainly wasn't shy about prying.

"I don't know," Doug muttered as he stared at his plate. "I haven't talked to them for a long time. They didn't … approve of some choices I made."

"That happens with families," Tilde said. "I definitely have my issues with some of the choices my sister has made. We're barely on speaking terms, but I keep trying for my niece's sake."

"It's good you keep trying for your niece," Nancy said. "I know it hasn't been easy for you."

"Well, she's worth it," Tilde said. "My sister on the other hand …" her voice trailed off and she shook her head disapprovingly.

Elias cleared his throat, his hand holding his wine glass swaying slightly. "I agree; it's really difficult when one of your siblings continues to mess up his life. Especially when the rest of the family doesn't see it."

"Oh, for the love of ..." Caleb muttered, rolling his eyes before turning to his brother. "Are you seriously going to keep this passive aggressive crap up all night? We get it. You're the perfect son and I'm the screwup. There, I said it. Can we finally move on now?"

"Boys, boys. Enough already ready," Ginny said with a sigh.

Elias slammed his wineglass down, ignoring his mother. The wine sloshed over the side, dribbling down the glass and onto the white tablecloth, leaving a thin, red trail. "No. We can't move on. Not until Mother knows the truth over what you did."

"Elias, what are you talking about?" Ginny asked. "Of course I know the truth."

Elias was shaking his head. "No, you don't. If you did, Caleb wouldn't be your favorite, the one you always wish was with you instead of the one who stuck by you all of these years."

"Elias." Ginny's voice was horrified. "That's not true. I love all my children equally."

"Hah," Miriam said, swallowing her wine and reaching for the bottle. "Apparently hell is freezing over because, for once, I agree with Elias. Caleb is definitely your favorite."

Caleb was staring incredulously at both of his siblings. "You guys are nuts. I'm the black sheep, not the favorite."

"You're the favorite," Elias said. "Although maybe you wouldn't be, if Mom knew the truth about what you did."

"Elias, I don't know what you're talking about," Ginny said. "Maybe you should slow down on the drinking."

"My drinking has nothing to do with the truth," Elias said, although his flushed face seemed to contradict him.

"Well, you're talking foolish," Ginny said.

"All you do is defend him," Elias said.

"I defend all my children," Ginny said. "That's what a mother does. But that doesn't mean I don't know the truth. I know Caleb got into the wrong crowd in high school, and that led to him making some bad choices."

"Oh, is that what you call killing someone? A bad choice?" Elias said.

There was a shocked silence. Elias looked around the table, his expression defiant, before reaching for the bottle to top off his wine glass.

"Elias, how could?" Ginny asked, her face white. "How could you lie about your brother like that?"

"It's not a lie. It's the truth." Elias said as he concentrated on pouring wine into his glass.

"It's a dreadful lie. Your brother didn't kill anyone," Ginny said.

"Then what happened to Willy?" Elias demanded. "After that day, he was never seen again."

Tilde made a choking noise in her throat. "Willy? That was really his name?"

"No, I think it was Will, or maybe Bill, but everyone called him Willy," Miriam said. "Dreadful nickname, isn't it?"

"I would say so," Tilde said. "I wonder what that poor boy did to get that nickname?"

"Why are you digging the past up?" Ginny asked. "He moved away. It was simple as that."

"The next day?" Elias asked. "No one does that."

"Nothing is ever simple in Redemption," Miriam said, sitting back in her chair as she swirled her wine in her glass.

"That's for sure," Tilde said.

"Do you think it's time for pie?" Nancy asked.

"Definitely. It's always time for pie," Tom said, getting to his feet and starting to collect the dirty plates. "You stay there.

"Why are you talking about your brother like he's not here?" Tilde asked Elias, oblivious to Nancy's and Tom's attempts to change the subject. "If you really think he killed someone, why don't you ask him?"

Total silence. Even Tom stopped collecting dishes and just stood there awkwardly, balancing a plate in each hand.

Caleb sat back in his chair and folded his arms across his chest. "Yeah, why don't you ask me?"

Elias's lips puckered up, like he had eaten something sour. "I guess I just assumed you wouldn't tell me the truth."

Caleb raised an eyebrow. "And you assume you know the truth?"

"You'd be surprised what I know," Elias said.

Caleb widened his eyes. "Oh, really? Why don't you enlighten us and tell us what you know?"

"Boys, this is not the time," Ginny said.

Elias ignored her and leaned forward toward his brother. "If you were innocent, why didn't you act innocent? Why didn't you say you didn't do it? That's what innocent people do."

"Why did I need to tell you, my brother, I was innocent?" Caleb demanded. "Why didn't you assume I was innocent without me having to tell you? Or, if that's too much, why didn't you ever ask me, instead of assuming because I didn't say anything I was guilty?"

"Enough!" Ginny slammed a hand on the table. "I'm sick of this bickering. It's Thanksgiving, we are with friends, and it's the first time we've been together in years. This is not the time or the place to dredge up the past. Got it?" She glared at both of her sons. Caleb dropped his head, an ashamed expression on his face. Elias just looked resentful as he took another sip of wine.

"Pie anyone?" Nancy asked, a forced note of cheerfulness in her voice.

"Absolutely," Tom said, immediately continued collecting dishes with a vengeance. The sound of the plates clanking together was so loud I wondered if he had cracked any. Nancy looked like she might be thinking the same thing, as I could see her wince a couple of times.

Ford had gotten to his feet and had picked up a few plates to carry to the kitchen. Doug also stood up. "I'll help, too."

"It's fine," Tom said as he walked by, balancing a stack of plates. His face was flushed, and I could see a line of sweat along his brow. "We've got it. You can help Caleb with the cleanup." He nodded toward Caleb.

Doug glanced uneasily at Caleb, as if he didn't relish the idea of spending time in a kitchen full of sharp knives with someone who had just been accused of murder. "What kind of pie does everyone want?"

"What? We have to choose?" Pat asked. "I wanted a piece of all of them." Tiki, who was on her lap, wagged her tail in agreement.

"Ditto," Wyle said. "It's Thanksgiving, after all. Bring all the pies out."

"I wouldn't have it any other way," Tom said, carrying a pie, but he didn't look right. His face was both flushed and pale, and the sweat was starting to soak through his brown sweater.

"Tom, are you okay?" Pat asked.

"I'm just … I'm not sure," Tom said, his voice sounded faint. He stumbled slightly. "All of a sudden, I just started to not feel good …"

"Hey, it's okay," Caleb said, standing up and taking the pie from him with one hand, and reaching for his arm with the other. "Why don't you sit down and …"

Right at that moment, there was a horrible crash coming from the kitchen.

"What the …" Caleb asked, turning away from Tom.

"Oh, no," Nancy gasped, jumping up. "Who's in the kitchen? Are you okay?"

"Is Ford in the kitchen?" Miriam asked, looking around.

"Ford?" Ginny repeated as she struggled to stand up. "Ford? Is that you in the kitchen?"

There was so much chaos at that point that everyone nearly missed Tom's eyes rolling at the back of his head before he collapsed in a heap.

Chapter 8

Pandemonium erupted. Chairs hit the floor as people jumped out of their seats. Everyone started shouting. A couple of people screamed. Tiki barked.

I dashed over to Tom, almost crashing into Doug, who was standing frozen in place, as if he couldn't process what was happening. I veered around him and nearly slammed into a shocked Nancy, who was also was just standing there. She was wringing her hands, seemingly unable to decide if she should run to the kitchen or see to Tom. "Pat, take Nancy into the kitchen to check out whoever is in there," I yelled as I flew by.

Pat, who had been matching my steps, nodded as she slowed down to take Nancy's arm. That seemed to jar Nancy out of her indecision. She blinked a couple of times and nodded before racing to the kitchen.

I knelt next to Tom, who was convulsing on the floor. Both Caleb and Wyle were next to me, and Caleb was trying to hold his head. "It happened too fast," Caleb was saying. "I couldn't get him."

"It's okay," I said, trying to adjust Tom's head and neck. "I don't think there was anything you could do."

"What's wrong with him?" Miriam asked, a hysterical note in her voice.

"Is he having a heart attack?" Elias asked.

"Wait a second. Where did Ford go?" Ginny said, her voice frantic.

"Maybe it was the food," Tilde said. "Although we all ate the same food. How are you feeling?"

"Tilde, you're not helping," I said, struggling with Tom, although I wasn't liking at all what I was seeing.

"He might be epileptic," Caleb said, then raised his voice. "Does anyone know if he's epileptic? Nancy, do you know?"

"Nancy is in the kitchen," I said, "but I think you should try the phones and see if you can call 9-1-1."

"Ford!" Ginny yelled. "Where are you? Ford?"

Wyle met my eyes. "Can you handle this?"

I nodded and Wyle stood up. "Everyone, please. This isn't helping," he said.

"But I don't know where Ford is," Ginny said.

"I think I saw him go into the kitchen," Tilde said.

"*He's* the one who ..." Ginny's voice trailed off, as if she couldn't bear to say the words. Or maybe it was more like if she didn't say them, they wouldn't come true. She pressed a hand over her mouth, as if that would keep them from escaping.

"I will go check the kitchen," Wyle said. "But everyone needs to take a breath."

"You need to call 9-1-1," I said to Caleb again. He was staring at Tom, his face slack with shock, and didn't seem to hear me.

I raised my voice. "Caleb!" He slowly lifted his head to look at me, and for a moment, I couldn't speak. His skin was so pale it looked bloodless, and his dark eyes were blank and empty. Was he about to collapse as well?

Then I remembered Tom, a man who I was fairly certain was dying right in front of me, unless we were able to get some help. Even if there was something wrong with Caleb, we needed to get the paramedics here. The sooner, the better. "Go try the phone again. Tom needs an ambulance. Do you hear me?"

Caleb stared at me for a moment, and then I saw the words finally penetrate. "Yes, of course. I'll go do that." He jumped to his feet and headed out of the room.

"What can I do?" Tilde asked, kneeling next to me where Caleb had been. She lightly touched Tom's face, and her brow furrowed. My heart sank. She could see it, too.

He wasn't going to make it.

"Pray," I said.

She glanced up, meeting my eyes briefly, before picking up one of Tom's hands and holding it between her own. She bowed her head.

There was another scream, this one coming from the kitchen. "Oh, no," Ginny said, her voice barely audible. "Ford." She seemed to have aged while sitting there. Wyle had made her sit back down before going into the kitchen to help, and looking at her, I was glad he did. She looked like she was about to faint. I glanced around the room to see if I could signal one of Ginny's kids, but Caleb had disappeared and both Miriam and Elias appeared to be as dazed as their mother. Miriam was staring into her drink, muttering something under her breath, her face pale under her heavy makeup, and Elias wasn't even looking in my direction but at something on the far wall.

I turned back to Tilde, who still had her head bowed. "Actually, once you're done praying, I have something else for you to do." Tilde raised her head, although her lips were still forming words. "Check on Ginny and make sure she doesn't fall out of her chair."

Tilde's eyes shifted toward Ginny. I saw them widen slightly once she saw what I saw, and she carefully tucked Tom's hand next to his body and moved over toward Ginny. I saw her put a hand on her shoulder and lean over to whisper in her ear.

"He's dead, isn't he?"

I did a double take. Miriam was looking at me with eyes as haunted as Caleb's had been, although hers was more bloodshot than his were. "Not if we get an ambulance here fast enough."

She let out a bark of laughter that had no humor in it. "Fat chance of that." She went back to staring at her drink. "This is our fault."

Her voice was so cold and dead it sent a shiver down my spine. "How is this your fault?"

"It's our family," Miriam said. "We're cursed."

That finally seemed to get Elias's attention. "Oh, stop it with the curse. We're not cursed, unless you count having the misfortunate to have been born and raised in Redemption. And having a sociopathic brother like Caleb." His voice was hard.

"What curse?" Tilde asked.

Miriam opened her mouth to answer, but Caleb walked into the room. "The phones are still dead."

"Of course they are," Miriam said.

"Maybe we should try and drive him to the hospital ourselves," Tilde said. "Do you think we can move him?"

"I don't think that's going to be possible either," Caleb said. "I checked outside, and it's really coming down. From what I can see, the roads look like they're a complete mess."

"But we can't just let him die," Doug said. His voice was hoarse, and I realized he hadn't moved from when I had nearly run him over from before. He was still staring at Tom, his eyes huge. "I can drive if no one else wants to."

"No one is driving in this weather," Caleb said. "If you get into an accident or drive into a ditch, that's not going to help anyone."

"But we can't just watch him die," Doug said. The candlelight had turned his skin gray, or maybe he was starting to feel sick as well. He swayed sightly like he was about to faint. "We have to do something."

"I'm not sure there's anything much we can do," I said, keeping my voice gentle. "Do you think you might want to sit down, Doug?" I thought about going to him, but I didn't want to leave Tom. Tilde caught my eye, and she gave Ginny's arm a squeeze and went over to Doug.

"But Ford?" Ginny asked. "Are we going to just let him die as well?" Even though she was now sitting, she didn't look much better than Doug did. I thought about the crash in the kitchen and started to get a sick feeling in my stomach. Had there been something in the food? Was the turkey not cooked properly?

Caleb's mouth flattened. "This is Tom we're talking about, not Ford."

"Then where is he?" She spread her hands out. "Something is going on in there," she jabbed her finger toward the kitchen, "and I haven't seen him since. Have you?"

"He's probably just in the bathroom or something," Caleb said.

"Or he's ransacking the hotel rooms," Elias muttered under his breath.

Ginny shot Elias a look, but before she could say anything, Wyle strode back into the room. Pat and Nancy trailed after him with Tiki running at Pat's feet. I caught Pat's eye, and I knew it was bad. My stomach twisted in an even tighter knot, and I was starting to wish I had skipped that extra helping of turkey.

"Everyone, I need you to remain calm. I have something to say, but first, how's Tom?" His eyes found mine, and I gave my head a quick shake. I could no longer feel a pulse and his chest had stopped moving.

I thought he might look more upset, or maybe come rushing over to see for himself, but instead he just looked resigned. "I was afraid of that."

Ginny was turning her head like she was watching a ping-pong match between us, and let out a little shriek. "Wait a minute. Are you saying … Tom is dead?"

"Unfortunately, it's not just Tom," Wyle said, his voice heavy.

Ginny gasped and pressed her hands to her mouth. "Ford is dead?"

"I'm afraid so," Wyle said.

"Oh, no," Ginny moaned, squeezing her eyes closed. "How? How did he die?"

"We're not sure," Wyle said, "but it seems to be similar to what happened to Tom." He nodded toward Tom.

"But that doesn't make any sense," Caleb said. "Ford wasn't an epileptic."

Wyle stared at Caleb, and I could see his what I called 'cop face' snap into place over his regular face like a mask. "Why do you think that Tom was an epileptic?"

Caleb's eyes widened. "I … uh … I don't. But it seemed like that's what happened to him. He had a seizure or something. Nancy, did you know if he was an epileptic?"

"I doubt it," Nancy said. "He never said anything to me about it, and Tom was pretty chatty. I feel like he would have said something."

"We could always check his room to see if he had medication," I said. "That would tell us for sure."

"That's not a bad idea," Tilde said. "It's not just epilepsy, but any underlying medical condition that might have caused this reaction."

"Although, that doesn't explain Ford, though," I said. "Unless they had the same underlying medical condition." I eyed Ginny, but she still looked like any second she was going to pass out. Luckily, Tilde was still hovering around her. Instead, I turned to the cousins. "Do you know if Ford was sick at all?"

"He never said anything to me about being sick," Caleb said.

"I wouldn't know," Elias said. "I haven't seen Ford in years."

"Really?" Even though it was off-topic, I couldn't help myself. "Why do you think he showed up for Thanksgiving today?"

"I haven't a clue," Elias said, giving his brother a sideways look. "Just like I haven't a clue why Caleb showed up today."

"Ford wasn't sick," Ginny said. She sounded calmer and the color was coming back to her cheeks, although maybe it was due to the glass of amber liquid she now held in her hand. Either Tilde or Nancy must have fetched it for her. "My sister would have said something." She squeezed her eyes tightly. "What am I going to say to her? How can I possibly tell her Ford is dead?" Her eyes suddenly popped open, and she looked hopefully at Wyle. "Are you sure he is dead? Maybe he's just … sleeping?"

"You mean like passed out?" Elias asked.

"Elias, what is wrong with you?" Ginny snapped. "Your cousin just died."

"So just because Ford is dead means we have to pretend he was a saint?" Elias asked. "We all know what kind of person he was."

Ginny's lips tightened in a thin line, but rather than answer Elias, she turned back to Wyle. "Or maybe Ford is just unconscious."

"I'm truly sorry for your loss," Wyle said.

Ginny closed her eyes again and took another sip of her drink.

Wyle glanced around the room, those cop eyes taking everything in. "So, I know this is all a big shock, and I wish things could be different, but unfortunately, I'm going to need to ask all of you some questions."

"Like what?" Miriam asked. "We already told you we don't know either Tom's or Ford's medical history. And we're not doctors, so how would we know what killed them?"

"It's true that we can't be completely sure about the cause of death until the M.E. has examined them," Wyle agreed, "and, with the weather the way it is, not to mention the phones still not working, I suspect we're not going to get him out here tonight."

"Wonderful," Elias said. "We're going to be stuck here all night with them."

"What?" Miriam let out a little shriek and put her wineglass down a little more sharply than she needed to. Out of the corner of my eye, I saw Nancy wince. "Wait a minute. Are you saying that we have to stay here with … two dead bodies?" She sounded horrified.

"Have you looked outside?" Caleb asked.

"I don't care." Miriam's voice was firm as she pushed herself to her feet, only wobbling slightly. "I am *not* spending the night here. Mom, let's go. Before the weather gets any worse."

Ginny was taking a sip of her drink and nearly choked. "Now? You want to go now? You know I can't drive when it's dark."

"I'll drive," Miriam said, taking a step forward. Actually, it was more like a stumble forward.

Wyle held both of his hands out. "No one is going anywhere."

Miriam gave him a defiant look. "You're not the boss of me. I can leave if I want."

Wyle's voice was calm. "No, you can't. The weather is way too bad for anyone to leave, but even if it wasn't, everyone needs to stay until the cops have done their initial investigation. Not to mention," he said, giving Miriam a stern look as she tried to talk over him, "you've had way too much to drink."

Miriam crossed her arms across her chest. "I'm fine. I can drive."

Wyle tilted his head. "Would you be able to pass a breathalyzer?"

"I agree with Wyle," Ginny said. "You're in no shape to be driving."

"Besides, like I said before, there's plenty of room here," Nancy said. "You can have your own room to sleep in tonight."

Miriam opened her mouth, then closed it when she seemed to realize she had lost the argument. "It's not like Mom lives very far," she muttered.

"It's not going to kill you to stay here for the night," Ginny said, then her mouth fell open as she realized what she just said. "Well, you know what I mean. And besides, we can't just leave Ford like that in the kitchen. He's your cousin. We have to make sure he's taken care of."

"I don't think Ford cares anymore," Elias said.

Ginny frowned at him. "Elias, I swear I don't know what's gotten into you."

"Can we at least not be in here?" Miriam asked, waving her hand toward Tom, who was still on the floor. "It's bad enough we have to spend the night with ... well, you know, but can we at least not have to sit here with them?"

"Good point," Wyle said. "We can go back to the lobby. That would probably be more comfortable for everyone."

"Maybe we can cover him as well," I said.

"Oh, yes, let's do that. For both of them," Nancy said, and hurried out of the room before Wyle could say anything.

"Everyone take a candle or a flashlight," Wyle said, but he needn't have bothered as everyone had already started grabbing them. Everyone, that was, except Miriam, who had picked up the wine bottle. Wyle cleared his throat, but Miriam was too busy filling her glass to notice. Once her glass was full, she tucked the bottle under her arm, picked up a candle with the other hand, and headed out of the room.

I met Wyle's eyes and shrugged. He rolled his eyes and went to help Ginny, who was trying to gather together a multitude of items to move into the lobby.

By the time Nancy had returned with a blanket to cover Tom, pretty much all of the candles had been moved to the lobby. I stayed behind to help Nancy cover him. With most of the light gone from the room, it was cast even more in shadow than before. The chairs and tables had morphed into dark creatures, crouching in the corners, just waiting for the rest of us to turn our backs and ...

I gave my head a quick shake. This was absolutely not the time to let my imagination run away from me. I had enough actual threats to worry about, and I didn't need to waste time thinking a random table was going to jump at me.

"I can't believe this is happening," Nancy said under her breath. Her face was pale, and there was a strained look around her lips. "One person would be a terrible tragedy, but two? And under these circumstances? And during Thanksgiving? What's going on?"

"I don't know," I said just as quietly, throwing a quick look over my shoulder to make sure no one was listening. It was so dark it was impossible to tell if someone was lurking in the corner, and I still didn't like the way those tables and chairs looked draped in darkness. "It does seem way too coincidental to be bad luck."

Nancy paused in the middle of covering Tom, her hands outstretched and the blanket trailing down like a curtain. "What are you saying?"

"I'm not sure," I said. "How well do you know Ginny and her family?"

She cocked her head. "You think Ginny had something to do with these deaths?"

"I have no idea, but her nephew is one of the victims, and her family is very ..." I hesitated, trying to think of a polite way of saying 'messed up'.

Nancy figured it out. "Dysfunctional?"

"Yeah. That works."

Nancy smiled slightly. "I've known Ginny for years. Her heart is in the right place, and Lord knows she tries, but, yeah ... her kids were certainly troubled in high school. Especially Caleb."

"Speaking of Caleb, what exactly happened in high school?" I asked.

She opened her mouth, but before she could answer, Wyle's voice boomed from the next room. "Charlie! Nancy! Are you going to join us?"

"Coming," I shouted back. "Just give us a second."

I turned back to Nancy with a shrug and a half smile, figuring she would tell me later, but Nancy's expression was deadly serious. "Whatever happens, know I'm on your side," she whispered.

The smile dropped from my face and the sick feeling that had lodged in my stomach intensified. "What?" I asked, but she was already heading into the lobby.

I watched her leave, an uneasy sensation prickling my skin, but I had no idea what I should do about it. For a moment, I pictured myself simply walking through the lobby to the front door and heading for home, but I knew there was no way I was going to do that. If nothing else, my curiosity was piqued, and now I wanted to know what was going on.

"Charlie?" Wyle yelled again.

"Hold your horses, I'm coming," I called back impatiently, then picked up the remaining two candles and followed her into the lobby.

"So, like I've been trying to tell all of you," Wyle was saying as we made our way into the lobby. He was standing near a table that was loaded with candles, but the light was hitting him from below, so his face was partially in shadow. Doug was crouched in front of the fireplace, poking at the fire, which had started roaring again. Everyone else had found somewhere to sit. Nancy went to the fireplace, and I headed toward Pat, who had saved me a spot on one of the loveseats. I did my best to not trip on anything or anyone as I picked my way toward her. She squeezed my hand as I sat down, and I noticed how cold it was. Even Tiki came over to give me a little kiss. I thought about how both Pat and Nancy had been alone in the kitchen with Wyle, and whatever was going on, I knew it wasn't good.

Maybe I should just head for my car after all.

"I know this isn't ideal," Wyle continued. "But since we're stuck here anyway, we might as well make the best of it. There are a number of things that don't … well, let's say, they don't quite add up."

"So what?" Elias said. "Why do we need to talk about it now? It seems to me that it would make more sense to talk about it tomorrow, after the cops have had a chance to look things over."

Wyle gave him a thin smile. "Well, that's the thing. I *am* a cop."

Chapter 9

"You're what?" Caleb was staring at him, a look of horror on his face. "You're a cop? Did the rest of you know that?" He whirled around the room.

"I didn't know, either," Doug said.

Elias shrugged. "Nor I. But what does it matter, brother? Unless you have something to hide?" He gave him a pointed smile.

"It's my fault," Nancy said quickly. "I should have done a better job introducing everyone. Yes, Wyle is an officer with the Redemption police department. I didn't think it mattered if Wyle was a cop or not. It's not like he was on duty tonight." She laughed a little, and then realized her mistake and quickly stopped. "Does anyone want anything more to eat or drink?"

"Yes," Elias said, making a show of pointing at his empty glass.

"If there's another bottle of wine somewhere," Miriam said, waving the bottle. "This is almost done."

"I don't think we need anything more right at this moment," Wyle said smoothly, as Nancy started bustling toward the makeshift bar, which still had plenty of bottles on it. "Maybe after we've answered a few questions, then we can see about opening another bottle."

"I still don't see why we need to be answering questions," Elias said. "No offense, I understand you're a cop, but it feels like we're putting the cart in front of the horse. We don't know what killed them, and we don't know their medical history, so I don't know how we can help."

"Humor me," Wyle said, with a smile which didn't reach his eyes. "We're not going anywhere, and with no electricity, we might as well talk, right?"

"So, what do you want to know?" Miriam asked impatiently. "Elias, we might as well answer the man's questions, and then we can get around to opening up more wine."

"Good point," Elias said.

"I want to know what are these things that don't add up," Tilde said.

"Yes, I think I'd like to know that, too," Caleb said. He had brought his glass to the lobby as well but, unlike his siblings, it didn't appear he had drunk much, if any, of it, as it was still half full. He regarded Wyle with a suspicious look. "What do *you* think is going on?"

"It is strange two people died," Tilde said before Wyle could answer. "If it had been only one, like Tom there, I would have thought maybe he had a heart attack or a stroke. He's at that age, and, well ..." she patted her stomach. "Let's just say he doesn't look like he misses too many meals, or lifts too many weights. But it wasn't just him. Ford was at least ten years younger and looked to be in pretty decent shape. It seems like it would be a stretch if they both died of a heart attack within minutes of each other."

"I agree," I said. "In fact, having them both die within minutes of each other does seem to rule a lot of options out." As much as I was hoping this would end up being a colossal accident or massive coincidence, I had a sick feeling in my stomach where this was going. Especially with how Wyle was acting.

Miriam turned to look at me. "What do you mean, rule a lot of options out? What are you trying to say?"

"What's she's saying," Wyle said, before I could decide if I should tell them where this was clearly going or if I should leave it up to Wyle. Luckily Wyle decided to step in, "is that it's probably not an accident."

Miriam turned to Wyle, her expression confused. "What do you mean, not an accident? Of course it's an accident. Or do you think they committed suicide?"

"Yes, Tom and Ford had formed a suicide pact," Elias said, rolling his eyes. "which is pretty amazing when you realize they just met tonight. That's what they must have been discussing when they were in the kitchen together."

Tilde snapped her fingers. "That's right. They were in the kitchen alone together. What do you think they were doing in there?"

"What, like forming a suicide pact?" Elias asked.

"No, I was thinking more like what if they ate or drank something they shouldn't," Tilde said.

"I told you, the turkey was done." There was an edge to Nancy's voice. "Just because my meat thermometer wasn't working doesn't mean I gave anyone food poisoning."

"I didn't say you gave anyone food poisoning," Tilde said.

"Besides, wouldn't we be all sick if that was the case?" Nancy asked, shooting Tilde a hard look.

I felt a shiver run down my spine, and my bad feeling about where this was all going got worse.

"I agree, we all did eat pretty much the same food," Tilde said. "That's why I was thinking maybe it was something they ate or drank that just affected *them.* Does anyone know if either of them had any allergies? Like food allergies?"

"Food allergies?" Ginny asked. "You think an allergy to food killed them?"

"Some food allergies can," Tilde said. "Peanut allergies and seafood are some of the worst."

"I don't think there was any seafood or peanuts in any of the food," Nancy said.

"It might not have been those specific foods," Tilde said. "I was just using those as an example."

"I doubt it's a food allergy," I said. "For the same reason, it probably wasn't a heart attack. Because it affected both of them. Again, it seems highly unlikely they would both have the same food allergy."

Tilde sighed. "That's true." She thought for a moment, tapping her finger on her lips. "Even if it wasn't a food allergy, it still could have been something they ate or drank while they were in the kitchen, which would explain why it only affected them and not the rest of us."

"Like what?" Elias asked. "Like drugs?"

"Tom didn't take drugs," Nancy said. "I would have known about that."

"Maybe it didn't come from Tom," Elias said. "Maybe Ford offered them to him, and he decided since it was a holiday, why not?"

"Ford wasn't doing drugs either," Ginny said.

"The hospital does have a strict no-drug policy," Tilde said. "Whether that extends to contractors or not, I'm not sure. I didn't think Tom was the type of guy would have wanted to risk all of these short-term contracts just for a little fun over Thanksgiving, but maybe. It would explain a lot."

Ginny was looking at Elias and Tilde incredulously. "I have no idea what Tom would or would not do, but Ford absolutely wouldn't be doing drugs in the kitchen during Thanksgiving while the rest of the family was in the other room. And he certainly wouldn't have *brought* any drugs to a family gathering. What is wrong with all of you?"

Elias was staring at her with an equally astonished expression on his face. "He did when he was a teenager. Or did you conveniently forget that?"

Ginny glared at him. "I didn't 'conveniently' forget anything. That was a long time ago, and he had gotten caught up with the wrong crowd. But, since then, he straightened himself out."

"How do you know this?" Elias asked. "Have you seen him recently?"

"I know," Ginny said. "I still talk regularly to your Aunt Jane. She keeps me up to date on Ford."

"If they're so close," Miriam said, slowly spinning the wineglass in front of her. "Why isn't Ford spending Thanksgiving with her? After all, she's his mother."

"I would imagine it's because Aunt Jane is in Florida this year for Thanksgiving," Ginny said stiffly.

"Mmm," Miriam said, her eyes still glued to her twirling wine glass. "And of course he was with her last Thanksgiving, right?"

Ginny suddenly became very busy with her own drink. "Probably, if they were both available. I can't remember that far back."

A small smile played on Miriam's lips, but she didn't answer.

"Well," Tilde said briskly after a short, uncomfortable pause. "If it was drugs that killed them, I'm sure the police will track down where they came from. Who knows, maybe they were left by another guest."

"What?" Nancy straightened up and put her hands on her hips. "First you criticize my cooking and now you're suggesting I'm running some sort of illegal flop house?"

Tilde looked taken aback. "What? No, of course not. I told you I didn't think it was food poisoning, but some sort of food allergies. And no, I don't think any of this is your fault. I know you wouldn't allow any drugs in here willingly, but people do all sorts of stupid things. It's possible a former guest had left something behind."

"If one of my guests was doing drugs, you can bet your bumpkins I would have done something about it," Nancy said, her expression even more miffed. "I would not tolerate drugs lying around …"

Wyle held up a hand. "I think we're getting a little off topic. Tilde is right; if it turns out there were drugs involved, at that point we'll investigate where they came from. But I do have a few other questions for everyone. Maybe it would be better if we did it privately. We could talk over there." He waved vaguely toward the other side of the hotel.

"Why would we want to talk privately?" Miriam asked, her voice full of suspicion.

"Well, maybe there's something you might not want to tell the group," Wyle said. "I don't want anyone to feel uncomfortable."

Miriam stared at him. "The only thing that would make me uncomfortable is going over there," she made a stabbing motion with her finger, "alone with you."

"If you want someone to come with you, that's certainly your prerogative," Wyle said.

"Is this an interrogation?" Miriam demanded. "What are you not telling us?"

"Miriam, you can't possibly be this stupid," Caleb said, "or has all the alcohol you've consumed over the years pickled your brain?"

She whirled on her brother. "Why would you say such a horrible thing to me? What's wrong with you?"

"What's wrong with *me*? You're the one who somehow hasn't grasped what's going on here," Caleb said.

Miriam put her hands on her hips. "Well, aren't you the smarty pants. So, tell us, oh wise one, what do you think is going on?"

Caleb gestured toward Wyle with his hand. "Isn't it obvious? He thinks Ford and Tom were murdered. And we're the suspects."

Chapter 10

For a moment, no one spoke or moved. The only sound was the crackling from the fireplace.

Ginny was the first to speak. "Did you say … murdered?"

"That's exactly what I said," Caleb said.

Miriam turned to Wyle. "You think one of us killed Ford and Tom?"

"But that can't be right," Ginny said with a little forced laugh. "Heavens, Caleb. You always had such an overactive imagination. Officer Wyle couldn't possibly think any of us are capable of killing anyone."

"Actually," Wyle said with a slight cough. "I think we're all capable of a great many things, depending on the circumstances."

"But why would any of us want to kill Ford or Tom?" Ginny asked. "That doesn't even make sense. We barely met Tom. And Ford, well, he's family."

"Yes, because we all know that no one ever kills another member of their family," Caleb said.

"Is that a confession?" Elias asked.

"Oh, don't be ridiculous," Ginny said. "Caleb isn't capable of murder. This is all just a big misunderstanding. I'm sure when the investigation is complete, it will be clear that whatever happened to Tom and Ford was a dreadful accident."

"I hope you're right," Wyle said gravely, "but, in the meantime, we need to explore all possibilities."

"Hold on," Miriam said, holding up a hand. "You're serious about this."

"There are several irregularities that need to be addressed," Wyle said.

Despite the warm light of the candles, Miriam's face looked greenish. "But if you're right, that means one of us is a killer, and you just said we can't leave. So that means we're trapped in this hotel *with a killer*?"

There was another moment of silence, this one longer than the first, as everyone uneasily eyed each other. I wondered if that was the real reason why no one had put the pieces together sooner, that they hadn't wanted to believe they had just eaten a Thanksgiving meal with a murderer.

"There's no need to panic," Wyle said. "We all just need to stay together and remain calm. I'm sure the phones will be working soon, and then we'll be able to get the police involved."

"You expect us to sit here twiddling our thumbs next to someone who murdered two people?" Miriam asked.

"I was hoping you could answer some questions," Wyle said, his voice mild.

Miriam rubbed her temples. "This is insane."

"You know," Tilde said, "it's possible it's not one of us."

Miriam stopped rubbing her temples and looked up. "What do you mean?"

"I mean, maybe there's someone else here," Tilde said. "In the hotel."

"What?" Ginny clutched at her sweater and looked right and left, as if she thought the killer would jump out of the shadows. "He's going to murder us all!"

"That's it. I'm outta here," Miriam said, stumbling slightly as she pushed herself to her feet. "I, for one, am not going to sit here and let someone pick us off one by one."

"So, you'd rather freeze to death outside," Elias said.

Miriam put a hand on her hip. "Actually yes. I *would* rather freeze to death outside."

"You're going to have to," Caleb said, "because you aren't going to be driving in this weather."

"I don't care," Miriam said over her shoulder as she stumbled to the front doors. "I'll walk if I have to."

"I don't think there's anyone else here," Nancy said.

"How do you know?" Ginny asked.

"Because I only have two other rooms rented, besides the two to Doug and Tom, and the guests from both of them left this morning to spend Thanksgiving with their families. I don't expect them back until later."

"But this is a hotel," Elias said. "A place of business. Anyone could have walked in, and if we were in the other room eating, we wouldn't have known it."

"That's why I lock the doors when I'm not actively working," Nancy said.

"What if your guests come back early and want to go to their room?" Elias asked.

"There's a bell near the front door with a sign asking them to ring if the door is locked," Nancy said. "We would have heard the bell. Wyle already asked me all of this earlier."

Miriam came stomping back across the lobby. "The front door is locked. I need you to unlock it."

Nancy gave her an uneasy look. "Wyle asked me to keep all of the doors locked ..."

Miriam stamped her foot. "I don't care what Wyle told you to do. I want out!"

"Miriam, please calm down," Wyle said.

"Calm down!" Miriam's jaw dropped. "You've locked me in a hotel with a murderer!"

"Not to mention that's probably a fire hazard," Elias said.

"Yes," Miriam said, pointing at Elias. "You're absolutely right. It *is* a fire hazard to have us locked in here like that. You're a cop," she said, whirling toward Wyle. "You should know that."

"You're not locked in," Nancy said. "First, I have the key on me so, if there were an emergency, I could unlock the door. And second, I have a fire exit in back. It's locked from the outside, so no, no one could have snuck in that way."

"And you're not going to go look for it," Wyle said, as Miriam's eyes went wide. "You're in no shape to go wandering around outside in the middle of an ice storm. So, just sit down, relax, and before you know it, the phones will be working again and we'll be able to call for backup."

"Maybe the phones will never be back," Miriam said, taking a step toward "Maybe whoever killed Tom and Ford cut the electricity and the phones. Did you think about that?"

Ginny let out a little shriek. "Oh, heavens! We really are going to be killed."

"No one is going to be killed," Wyle said, holding his hands out before turning back to Miriam. "Let's do this. You stay and answer some questions. And if the phones and the electricity aren't back by the time we're all ready to turn in, we can have another conversation about you leaving. Okay?"

"You might as well stay," Caleb said. "You know all this insisting that you want to leave just makes you look guilty, don't you?"

Miriam looked aghast. "You think I killed Ford and Tom?"

"I didn't say what I think," Caleb said. "I was merely telling you how it looks to the cop. You protest too much, my dear sister."

Miriam opened her mouth, then closed it, then gave both Caleb and Wyle a hard look. "Fine." She plopped back down. "I'll stay and answer your questions. But," she pointed her finger at Wyle, "if anything happens to me, I'm going to hold you personally responsible."

"Fair enough," Wyle said, "and, to be clear, we're considering all options, including that there might be someone else in the hotel."

Miriam sat back in her chair, arms crossed over her chest, a sour expression on her face. Elias looked bored, but I had a niggling feeling that was more of an act that what he really felt. Ginny, however, looked terrified. She was still clutching her sweater and her eyes were darting around the room, as if she was just waiting for someone to jump out of the shadows. On the complete opposite end of the spectrum, Tilde had the excited look children get on Christmas morning, as if she couldn't believe her luck that she was finally part of a real police investigation.

Nancy and Pat both seemed more guarded. Tiki gave me another kiss, which somehow heightened my concern rather than allayed it.

Caleb and Doug, however, I couldn't quite read. They both seemed very interested in what Wyle was saying, and were both watching him carefully, but both of them also seemed to be hiding their real feelings. Doug was probably wishing he had never left his room, but I couldn't read Caleb. There was something going on with him. How strange was it that he had decided to come back for Thanksgiving now after all of these years, and two people just happened to die?

Something wasn't quite right.

"But, first, I just have a few questions," Wyle said. From somewhere, he had produced a small notepad and pen. I thought I recognized the Redemption Inn logo on the notepad, but I couldn't be sure. He clicked the pen. "I was hoping we could get a rundown as to who was in the kitchen and when."

"The kitchen? Well, that's easy," Miriam said, crossing her legs. "I wasn't in the kitchen at all."

Wyle was busy taking notes. "Not once tonight?"

"Not once," Miriam said. She was swinging the leg that was crossed in an almost frenzied way that struck me as odd. When Caleb had first brought up that her insistence on leaving was making her look guilty, I had dismissed it, mostly because I didn't blame her for wanting to leave. I wanted to leave, too, and I knew I wasn't guilty.

But, watching her leg violently twitch, it made me start to second guess that.

"How about you?" Wyle said, looking at Elias.

"Me?" Elias seemed surprised to be asked. "I wasn't in the kitchen, either. Trust me, no one wants me anywhere near a stove."

"I guess that means you're not going to be eating much, now that you're divorced," Miriam said waspishly.

Elias turned beet red. "I'm perfectly capable of fending for myself." His tone was formal.

Miriam rolled her eyes. "If you say so."

"Caleb, how about you?" Wyle asked, cutting off Elias just as he was about to respond. "Were you in the kitchen at any point?"

"I carried in the wine we brought," Caleb said, shifting in his chair.

Wyle made a note. "Doug?"

Doug cleared his voice. "Just to bring the pies out, right before … all of this happened."

Wyle turned to Ginny and Tilde. "What about you two?"

"Well, I carried my dish into the kitchen," Tilde said. "Mashed potatoes, gravy and rolls. All from scratch."

"I did, too," Ginny said. "The sweet potato casserole."

"Was that all?"

"Well, no, I was in and out helping Nancy," Ginny said.

"Do you remember when?"

"No, I didn't keep track. Why would I keep track of how often I was in the kitchen?" Ginny asked.

"Were you ever in there alone?" Wyle asked.

"Why are you asking all of these questions?" Elias asked. "What happened in the kitchen? What aren't you telling us?"

"What about when the lights were out?" Wyle asked. "Did anyone go into the kitchen then?"

"I have no idea where I was. I was too busy looking for candles and flashlights," Elias said.

"I bet it was drugs," Tilde said. "Did you find drugs on Ford?"

"It wasn't drugs," Wyle said.

"Of course it wasn't," Ginny said. "I told you; Ford doesn't do drugs."

"Well, something killed him," Tilde said. "If it wasn't drugs, then what was it?"

"I still want to know why Wyle kept asking if we were in the kitchen or not," Elias said.

"I'll get to that in a moment," Wyle said. "Doug, you said the only time you went into the kitchen was to bring the pie out, correct?"

"That's right," Doug said.

"Did you sneak a bite for yourself?"

Doug looked floored. "What?"

"Seriously?" Miriam asked. "You're like the dessert police now?"

"There's a method to my madness," Wyle said, still looking at Doug. "It's Thanksgiving. If there's ever time to cheat a little on your diet, it's today, right?"

"I don't eat pie," Doug said stiffly. "I already blew my diet enough today, I had decided I wasn't going to have any pie."

Wyle tilted. "No pie? Then why were you bringing it out?"

Doug's eyes darted around the room. "I was trying to help out. Tom and Ford had done so much, and I thought it was the least I could do. Why? Is there something wrong?"

"I'm not sure yet," Wyle said, looking at Caleb. "How about you? Did you have any pie?"

"Why would I have any pie?" Caleb asked. "All that would do is spoil my appetite for turkey."

"Did anyone have any pie?" Wyle asked, looking around the room.

I couldn't stand it anymore. My stomach had turned into an icy knot. "Why are you asking about my pies?" I burst out. "Is there a problem with them?"

Wyle turned to me, then, and I saw something in his eyes: a reluctance, or maybe an apology. "When you brought the pies, did you have a piece at home?"

"No, of course not," I said. "Why would I do something like that?"

"Maybe to taste it, to make sure it was up to your standards?"

"It's never even occurred to me to do that," I said. "Why? Was there a piece missing?"

Wyle bent his head at the same time Pat squeezed my hand again. "It appears that someone had started dessert early."

"And you think it was one of us?" Miriam asked.

"That's why I'm asking. Did anyone have any pie?"

There was a moment of awkward silence as everyone shook their head and looked at everyone else. The cold lump in my stomach had started radiating outward, and now my whole body was turning to ice. This couldn't be happening. Wyle couldn't be saying what I thought he was saying. Pat reached over and squeezed my hand again, and my heart sank further.

It was exactly what I was afraid it was.

"Maybe there's a mouse in the kitchen that got into the pie," Miriam said.

Nancy straightened up. "There are absolutely *no* mice in my kitchen right now."

"What about Tiki?" Ginny asked. "Could she have gotten into it?"

Tiki sat up and let out a little a little squeak in indignation.

"It was on the counter," Pat said, "and she's a toy poodle. How is she possibly getting up there alone?

"Which pie was it?" Tilde asked.

"Mincemeat," Wyle said.

Tilde's eyes widened. "Mincemeat! Oh, who was it that was so excited to have mincemeat because their grandmother used to make it. Doug, was it you?" She turned to Doug.

"I told you, I don't eat pie," Doug said.

"Oh, then it must have been …" Tilde's brow furrowed as she paused in thought. I saw the moment she connected the dots, as her expression suddenly changed to shock.

"Ford said that," Miriam said quietly.

"And Tom," Elias added.

"And they were both joking about starting dessert early," Miriam said.

"And they were alone in the kitchen together," Elias said.

There was another uncomfortable pause before everyone turned to stare at me.

Chapter 11

"Even if they both did eat the pie, so what?" I said. "There was nothing in the pie that would have killed them."

"But no one else ate the pie but them," Elias said. The flames from the candle emphasized the shadows of his face, giving him an almost eerie look. "And they're both dead."

"If that's the case, it's a coincidence," I said. Despite how cold I was, I could feel drops of sweat start to trickle down my back.

"That's one heck of a coincidence," Elias said.

Miriam's mouth was hanging open. "What did you put in the pies?"

"Just what you would expect," I said. "Eggs, vanilla, sugar. Lots of sugar."

"Wait a minute," Tilde said. "You're not saying you think Charlie had anything to do with Ford and Tom's death? That's ridiculous."

"I agree," Nancy said. "Charlie wouldn't hurt a fly."

"We're not saying it," Elias said, gesturing toward Wyle. "He's the one saying it."

Wyle held a hand up. "Hold on. I'm not accusing anyone of anything. I don't know who or what killed Tom and Ford. That's why I'm asking questions."

"It sure sounds like you're saying Charlie killed Tom and Ford," Elias said. "She baked the pie that they ate, and now they're dead. That seems pretty clear-cut to me."

"I didn't kill Tom or Ford," I said. "There was nothing wrong with that pie."

"Maybe there was something in it they were both allergic to," Tilde said. "What's in a mincemeat pie, anyway?"

"Apples, raisins, brandy, currents, almonds, a bunch of spices," I said.

Tilde raised her eyebrows. "That does sound good."

"I thought mincemeat had beef in it," Nancy said.

Miriam's forehead creased. "Beef? In a pie? Yuck."

"That was how they used to make it a hundred years ago," I said. "Now it's normally fruit, nuts and spices."

"Man, I'd love to taste it," Tilde said.

"No one is tasting any pies," Wyle said, while shooting me an apologetic look.

"Well, yes. Understandably," Tilde said, but not without a touch of disappointment. She gave herself a quick shake. "Anyway, what about the almonds? Plenty of people have a nut allergy, so maybe that's what killed them."

"I think Tom would have mentioned a nut allergy to me," Nancy said. "Some of the muffins I make in the morning have nuts in them."

"I'm sure Ford doesn't have a nut allergy," Ginny said.

"I'm having trouble believing either one of them had a serious food allergy," I said, even though a part of me almost wished that could be the explanation. Not that I wanted to have had any part of their deaths, but if it was a food allergy that I didn't know about, while their deaths would still be a terrible tragedy, it would be an accident. We wouldn't be eying each other, wondering if there was a killer sitting among us or lurking around in the dark corners. At this point, I couldn't decide which would be worse. "The people I've known who have been allergic to a food usually would ask if any of the dishes contain it. Neither Ford nor Tom asked, so I don't think a food allergy can explain what happened to them."

"Exactly," Nancy said. "People want you to know their food allergies if you're preparing meals for them."

Miriam was staring at me again. "So, if it wasn't an accident, then you must have killed them on purpose."

"What?" I couldn't believe what I was hearing. "You seriously think I killed Tom and Ford?"

Miriam shrugged. "It sure seems like you did. Who brings a mincemeat pie to a Thanksgiving meal, anyway?"

"Someone who had to make multiple pies and already had two pumpkins and a pecan," I said.

"And it just happens to be Ford and Tom's favorite pie?" She narrowed her eyes as she studied me, reminding me of a cat that was getting ready to pounce on an unsuspecting mouse. "That's a pretty big coincidence, wouldn't you say?"

"Oh, for heaven's sake," I said impatiently. "Why would I kill either one of them? First of all, I had no idea either one of them would be here today —"

"Nancy didn't tell you about Tom?" Miriam asked.

"She told me there would be two of her guests, but she didn't tell me their names," I said. "Why would she? The chances of me knowing them were slim to none."

"So you say," Miriam said.

"Did it seem like Tom and I knew each other?" I asked sarcastically.

Miriam held her hands out, palms up. "I have no idea. I'm just saying bringing mincemeat pie is odd enough, and the fact it just happens to be the favorite pie of two people *who died* is very suspicious."

I couldn't believe I was having this argument. "Well, all I can tell you is I didn't know who Tom was. As for Ford, I didn't even know he existed until I showed up here, pie in hand."

"Charlie, can I talk to you for a second?" Wyle asked, gesturing with his head toward the corner of the room.

Miriam gave me a triumphant smile that looked like a cat who had just drank the cream. I stood up, trying to keep my legs from shaking. Even though I knew I had nothing to do with Tom and Ford's death, I had to agree that Miriam had a point. It *was* very strange that of all the pies I could have chosen; I picked a pie that was a favorite of two men who apparently died after eating it. If I were in Miriam's shoes, I would be suspicious of me as well.

Maybe I should have made a lemon pie after all.

Wyle led me to a corner of the room, far from the candlelight. His face was shadowed in darkness as he turned toward me. We were close enough I could smell him, that mixture of his soap and shampoo with his unique scent. "I have to ask. What's going on with your pies?"

"Nothing is going on with my pies," I said. "I baked them exactly the way I bake everything, and no one has ever gotten sick from my baking."

"Other than today, that is," Wyle said.

"If it even *is* my pie," I said. "We haven't proved either Tom or Ford ate my pie, much less that was what killed them."

"True, but in the meantime, why don't you tell me what happened when you were baking today," Wyle said.

"The same that always happens," I said. "I mixed together flour, butter, salt and water for the crust, all the pies got the same recipe for the crust, and then I worked on the fillings, which while all of them were different, there were some similarities such as lots of sugar, vanilla …"

"I meant did anything happen while you were baking?" Wyle cut in. "Like, was anyone there? Did you leave at any time?"

"I did leave for a quick grocery store run," I said, "but that was before I started the mincemeat pie. Nancy had called me to ask me to bake more pies, and I decided mincemeat might be fun, but I needed a few more ingredients."

"Could anyone have snuck in and tampered with your ingredients?" Wyle asked. "Like maybe your sugar?"

"I didn't notice anything," I said, but then I wondered if I would have. I was in a hurry making those final two pies, so I would have just measured ingredients and dumped them into the bowl.

"But it's possible," Wyle pressed.

"I suppose," I said slowly as the ramifications of what he was saying started to sink in. The cold that had lodged in my stomach began to radiate outward, freezing my organs in the process. "You really think someone broke into my house while I was gone so they could poison either Ford or Tom? That just seems so … farfetched. How did they even know I was going to bake more pies? How did they know I was going to be here for Thanksgiving? Or that Ford and Tom were going to be here?"

Wyle's lips were pressed in a straight line. "I don't know. I agree it's farfetched, but is it any more farfetched than you deliberately poisoning one of the pies?"

"Well, when you put it that way," I said, "but still: if they wanted to kill Ford or Tom, don't you think there would be an easier way? An awful lot had to go right for this plan to work."

"You're assuming either Tom or Ford was the target," Wyle said, his voice flat.

For a moment, my heart seemed to stop beating. I stared at him, feeling sick, as images of my lovingly baked pies filled my head. Sweet, delicious pies that may be full of poison. "So," I said when I finally found my voice. "You think maybe I was the target? Someone was trying to kill me with my own pies?"

"Or trying to set you up," Wyle said. "Either way might work for them, if you were the target."

I briefly closed my eyes. There were two people in town, Louise and Rowena, who I knew would like nothing better than to see me pack up and go. Louise had been one of my first friends when I had moved to town, but a couple of months after I arrived her brother disappeared. To this day, she blamed me for his disappearance, even though most people told her she was being irrational. I had a feeling deep down she really blamed herself, because she and her brother had had a huge fight right before he disappeared, but it was easier to blame me.

Rowena was a little different story. She had claimed to be a psychic and had opened up a shop in downtown Redemption. However, I knew she was a fake, and she knew I knew she was fake. We had clashed a couple of times, and I knew she had tried a few times to get me to leave, but nothing had stuck.

But still, trying to drive me out of town was one thing, and committing murder was a completely different ball game. I couldn't see either of them breaking into my house and sabotaging my pies.

"It's possible, however, you might not be the target," Wyle said, and I opened my eyes. "It's possible it's one of them." He nodded toward the rest of the group.

"Again, though, how would whoever did this know I was going to be here today? Or that I would be bringing pies?"

A small smile touched his lips. "Charlie, of course you're going to be bringing pies. What else are you going to bring?"

I had to admit he had a point.

"However, again, it's possible this isn't about you at all, but someone else here. If that's the case, it's possible they did some digging on their own. Maybe they were even specifically looking for whoever was baking the pies, and it just happened to be you."

"Maybe," I said, throwing a glance over my shoulder to look at the rest of the group. They were still seated in the same place as before, although they weren't talking much. I saw Miriam take a sip from her glass and realized she and Elias had managed to find a bottle of wine while I was talking to Wyle. "This whole thing is surreal."

"It will be better once we can call it in," Wyle said. "Once we can pinpoint what killed Tom and Ford, it's going to be a lot easier to focus. Right now, there's too many variables."

"Yeah, I agree." My eyes had fallen on Caleb, who was playing with his wineglass. His dark hair fell across his forehead and nearly in his eyes. There was something about him, a broodiness maybe, that set him apart from his siblings.

Was that the source of bad blood between them? Although, to be fair, Elias and Miriam also were at each other's throats, although neither of them were accusing the other of murder.

What had happened in that family that had created so much animosity? While it was true lots of families didn't get along, this seemed to take that to another level. Was it just normal fights and disagreements that had never gotten resolved?

Or had something even worse happened?

And why would Caleb, after all this time, choose to come back now? He must have known what he would be walking into. Why this day?

And if he hadn't come back, would Ford and Tom still be alive?

Chapter 12

"I want to see the kitchen," I said abruptly.

Wyle looked a little taken aback. "I don't know if that's a good idea," he said.

"It's not a good idea; it's a great idea," I said. "My pies are being slandered. I have the right to see the crime scene. My pies and I have a right to defend ourselves."

Wyle didn't seem so sure. "That may be true, but it's also important to not contaminate the crime scene. It's bad enough that everyone was in the dining room when Tom collapsed. I'm trying to at least keep the kitchen as pristine as possible, especially if it turns out that was where the murders took place."

"What if I promise not to touch anything?" I asked.

"It's better if we stay out of that room," Wyle said. "I know it's difficult but—"

"Wyle," I interrupted, "I've been at crime scenes before. I know the drill. I also know there might be something in there, some clue, that other people might miss. You know I'm good at picking up details like that."

"I don't know," Wyle said hesitantly. "Even going into the room can contaminate it."

"If you're worried about a strand of my hair falling on the floor or my fingerprints getting on the counter, you shouldn't be," I said. "I've already been in the kitchen earlier today, so you could argue I've already contaminated the scene."

"It's going to be difficult to see anything in the kitchen with the lights off," Wyle said, but I could tell he was starting to relent.

"That's what flashlights are for," I said. "I agree it isn't ideal, but none of this is ideal. We may be trapped in a hotel with a killer. Is that ideal? The least we can do is arm ourselves with as much knowledge as possible so we can defend ourselves, wouldn't you agree?"

Wyle stared at me for a long moment, then let out a long breath before glancing over my shoulder at the rest of the group. "We shouldn't leave them alone for very long."

"We won't," I said. "I'm just asking for a few minutes to see the crime scene. I won't touch anything, I'll use my flashlight to look around, and I'll be quick. Okay?"

Wyle made a face. "You better make it quick."

"I promise."

He sighed and turned to lead me toward the kitchen, but before he opened the door, he paused, his hand in the middle of the wood paneling. "I just want it on the record that I don't think this is a good idea."

"Noted. And the sooner you let me in, the sooner we'll be out."

He gave me an unreadable look, before shaking his head and pushing the door open.

I stepped inside and started moving the beam of the flashlight around the room. The first thing I saw was Ford still lying on the floor. Unlike Tom, he hadn't been covered. I quickly shifted the light away and started searching the rest of the kitchen.

"Seen enough?" Wyle asked from behind me.

"I barely started," I said impatiently and took a step forward.

The kitchen was still fairly tidy, with only one pile of dirty dishes next to the sink. My pies had also been unwrapped. One of the pumpkin pies had what looked like three pieces removed, and the other pumpkin and the pecan pie were untouched. Next to the pumpkin that was being served was a stack of small plates with a piece of pie on the top one. Next to the plates was a dirty knife and spatula.

Tucked in the corner was the mincemeat, also with a piece removed.

"I see why you thought it was the mincemeat," I said, taking a step closer to the counter. "Tom brought out pieces of pumpkin pie, didn't he? So, it looks like all pumpkin pieces are accounted for, but not the mincemeat."

"Exactly," Wyle said. He had moved to stand next to me. "Which isn't to say the other pies aren't tainted. We won't know for sure until we test them all, but it appears the only one that was eaten was the mincemeat."

"It does seem that way," I said, running my flashlight over the counter. On closer inspection, I noticed the kitchen wasn't nearly as clean as Nancy had left it. There was a trail of crumbs across the counter, and the garlic press was wedged between the dirty plates and the splash guard. Some of the silverware had fallen into the sink, along with the mortar and pestle and turkey baster.

"Now are you satisfied?" Wyle asked.

"Not yet," I said, running the flashlight more slowly along the counter. Something wasn't right, but I couldn't put my finger on what it was. I moved my flashlight to look into the sink, and saw that the mortar was full of water.

"This is different," I said.

Wyle craned his neck over my shoulder. "What's different?"

"The dishes here." I waved my hand over the sink.

He looked at me sideways. "You think there's a problem because someone put dirty dishes in a sink?"

"No, it's not that. Before dinner, Nancy had the mortar and pestle and the turkey baster next to the sink. With the garlic press." I shone my light toward the garlic press.

He looked at the garlic press, then back at me. "Well, maybe whoever brought the dirty plates in here wanted more room, so they moved those into the sink."

"But, why? Why not just push it over like they did the garlic press? There was plenty of room on the counter. They could have pushed them over this way," I gestured toward the opposite side of the sink. "Or just left them alone. There was really no reason to move them."

Wyle shone his own flashlight around. "It seems a little weak," he said finally. "I see what you mean, but someone moving a couple of dirty dishes into the sink isn't a big deal."

"But they also rinsed them off," I said, moving my flashlight around the puddle of water in the mortar. "Why would they bother to do that? I can see what you mean by moving them, but why take the extra step to rinse them?"

"Maybe they didn't mean to. They turned the water on for another reason," Wyle said, moving the flashlight. "Maybe …" he voice suddenly altered. "What's that?"

I directed my flashlight to where he was looking. "It looks like … is it a used match?"

We both took a step closer to the sink. There, right next to the drain, was a small, piece of cardboard that was burned black.

"Was anyone in here looking for matches or a flashlight?" I asked.

Wyle was still staring into the sink. "I don't think so. Nancy was directing everyone to the storage closet in the hallway along with that chest of drawers for candles and flashlights. Not the kitchen."

I looked at the burned match. "It's possible Tom or Ford lit a match."

"Possible," Wyle said, "although I'm pretty sure they both had their own flashlight."

"Yeah, I thought I remembered that, too," I said, thinking back to watching Tom juggling a flashlight and an armful of dirty dishes. "Which doesn't mean they didn't light a match in here."

Wyle had a thoughtful expression on his face. "No, and it might be why they decided to turn the water on, to make sure the match was out."

"Possibly, but …" My voice trailed off. I couldn't describe it, but it still didn't feel right to me. It was a small thing, granted, but sometimes it was the small details that ended up tripping us up the most.

Wyle turned away from the sink. "We should get back out there. We've left them alone long enough."

"Yeah, you're probably right," I said, taking one last look at the match as I followed him out of the swinging door.

"Everything okay between you lovebirds?" Elias called out when he saw us.

I could feel my face flush and was glad of the darkness that hid it.

"Everything is fine," Wyle answered back, his voice short. "Just checking on something."

"Uh *huh*," Elias said.

"So that's what they call it now," Miriam said, and both of them laughed.

Wyle gave his head a quick shake before turning back to me. "We need to wrap this up and get back to the group," he said, his voice low.

I was still thinking about the kitchen, the dishes in the sink, the burned match, and the piece missing from the mincemeat pie. "This is what I keep coming back to," I said, "we really have no idea what happened in that kitchen. None whatsoever."

Wyle paused and tilted his head. "True."

"Ford and Tom could have been doing drugs for all we know," I continued. "Maybe they were smoking heroin, and that's why they needed a match."

"I think we would have smelled it if they were smoking dope."

"Maybe. Probably." I gestured with my hand, "but what I'm trying to say is we still have a lot of questions and no answers."

Wyle chewed on his lip. "You have a point. When you first look around the kitchen, it does appear that Tom and Ford decided to try the pie and that's what ended up killing them. But is that true? Was it just an innocent mistake on their part, because the pie was meant for someone else? Or was it something else they ate or drank?"

"You know, it doesn't have to be the pie," I said thoughtfully. "Some poisons take hours or even days before they kill you. Ricin is one. Is it possible they were the target, after all, but someone poisoned them a day or two ago?"

Wyle considered that. "You mean like they actually knew each other before today and were just pretending they had just met? That's interesting."

"I mean, what do we truly know about either Ford or Tom? Other than they magically clicked. Is it possible they were already friends and maybe even hung out together earlier this week, and that was when they were poisoned?"

Wyle tapped the cover of his notebook, as if he were trying to decide if he should write a note for himself or not. "It is true that I was assuming Tom wasn't the target. He was a mistake, at the wrong place at the wrong time. But, if he *was* the target ..."

"If that's the case, maybe Ford was the one who was a mistake," I said. "Speaking of which, do we know where either of them were last night? I know we're limited to the people here in this room, but maybe we should see if we can trace their steps."

"Yeah, I think that's a good idea." Wyle flipped open his notebook and started scribbling again. "I don't know how far we'll get, but we can at least try."

"Maybe you should ask Nancy if we can, or at least *you* can, search Tom's room," I said.

Wyle made a face. "I would have, but with the electricity out, it didn't seem to make a lot of sense. Searching with a flashlight is difficult under the best of conditions, and this is definitely not that. Plus, I didn't want to leave all of you alone, in case something … happened."

I didn't like the sound of that. I glanced over my shoulder again and lowered my voice. "Are you saying you think we're in danger?"

"No," Wyle said quickly. A little too quickly. His eyes darted behind me, as if he was also keeping an eye on the group of people behind us.

"But, if one of them is the killer …" I said.

"If one of them is the killer, then I suspect it's probably personal," Wyle said. "I doubt they would suddenly go on a murder spree. If this is about you and you were the target, either to discredit you or … hurt you, then the killer wouldn't be in the room and there's no danger."

"But what if the killer isn't part of our group, but *is* in the hotel with us?" I asked.

Wyle's eyes hardened. "I think that's the least likely scenario, but yes, you should definitely stay alert and be aware of your surroundings, especially while the electricity is out, but also until the phones come back and we can get some backup out here."

"Understood," I said, trying not to shiver. I really didn't like the idea of someone lurking in the shadows, watching us and maybe waiting for their chance to leap out and attack. "I'll let Pat know as well. Maybe we can use Tiki to check if there's someone there."

I was half joking, but Wyle seemed to be taking me seriously as he shot me an exasperated look. "I don't think a toy poodle is going to be much of a help in this situation."

"Well, it might be better than nothing," I said, with half of a smile. "You never know. Poodles were known as hunting dogs."

Wyle didn't look amused. "Charlie, I'm serious. You need to remain vigilant."

"I got it, I got it," I said, trying not to roll my eyes. "Can I be excused now?"

Wyle stared at me for a long moment before giving me a quick nod. I started to turn away, but he called my name. "Just be careful. I know you're going to be asking a lot of questions, and I stand by what I said earlier, if it is someone in this room, I don't think you're in a danger, but ..." He hesitated for another moment. "Just keep in mind you're still dealing with a killer. Okay?"

"I'll be careful. Promise."

He didn't look convinced, but after another look behind me, he nodded briefly and took a step back.

Chapter 13

I headed back to my seat next to Pat. A couple of people had been talking in low voices, but that ceased as I picked my way across the lobby. I could feel their eyes burning a hole in the center of my back, but I forced myself to move as normally as possible. Other than the sounds of the fire crackling and the wind whistling outside, it was eerily silent. "What did Wyle say?" Pat whispered in my ear as I settled in next to her.

"Tell you later," I whispered back.

Tiki nosed my hand and gave me a concerned look. I petted her behind her ears.

Out of the corner of my eye, I could see Miriam watching me. I waited for her to say something, but she turned to Wyle instead. "Are you arresting her yet?" Miriam asked.

Wyle pulled a chair over and sat down. "No one is getting arrested. I told you we have to wait until we can call it into the station and get a team over here. There's a lot of evidence we're going to need to process."

"Hmph," Miriam said, narrowing her eyes. "Then what were you two talking about all cozy over there?"

"Well, I thought rather than waiting for the police, we'd just use Tiki here to start tracking down evidence," I said, rubbing her chin. "Your nose can probably tell us a lot, can't it?"

Tiki wagged her tail.

"See. Tiki agrees," I said. "If there is someone hiding out in the hotel, Tiki will find them, won't you?"

Tiki wagged her tail harder. Miriam rolled her eyes.

"Not only that, she'll look fabulous while doing it," Pat said proudly, straightening her turkey sweater.

"That's not a bad idea," Tilde mused. "Maybe we should let the dog explore the hotel and see what she finds."

"We are not letting a dog the size of a hamster wander around a dark hotel," Wyle said.

"But she's a poodle," Tilde said. "Poodles are hunting dogs."

"She's a *toy* poodle," Wyle said. "Very different."

"While I agree we shouldn't use the dog," Caleb said, eying Tiki, who was still wagging her tail proudly as she basked in all the attention, "searching the hotel isn't a bad idea. Maybe we should divide up into groups and look around, just to make sure there isn't anyone else here."

"Caleb is right," Elias said, "and I don't say that very much, but I, for one, feel like a sitting duck right now. We should be on the offense, not the defense."

"I think it would be best if we stayed here," Wyle said smoothly. "Not only is there safety in numbers, but walking around in an unfamiliar building in the dark isn't the wisest move. There's always a possibility someone could get hurt. Someone could trip, fall down the stairs, you name it, and we don't need any more emergencies than we already have."

"So, you just want us to sit here and twiddle our thumbs while we wait to be attacked?" Elias asked.

"I don't think we're going to be attacked," Wyle said. "Like we said earlier, I think it's a very remote possibility that someone else is in here with us."

"I'm not sure that's particularly comforting," Miriam said. "While it's true a murderous stranger would be bad, it might be just as bad to discover one of us is the murderer."

There was a long pause as we all stared uneasily at each other. I could feel the situation was fast deteriorating, and based on Wyle's tight expression, it seemed he could feel it too.

"You know, I'm curious how everyone ended up in Redemption," I said, breaking the stillness. "Am I the only one who didn't grow up here?"

"I didn't," Wyle said, "but you already know that."

"That's true," I said. "I guess me and Wyle."

"And me," Doug said. "This is my first time in Redemption. Might be my last, too." He took a long sip of wine.

"Well, I've been here all my life," Tilde said. "Born and raised."

"Same here," Pat said.

"My family moved here when I was a child, so I feel like I've lived here forever," Nancy said.

"I've lived here my entire life," Ginny said, "although my children haven't." She shot them all a hard look.

"Who would want to stay here if they didn't have to?" Miriam asked with a shiver.

"Exactly," Elias said. "As I said before, this place is cursed."

"Redemption was a lovely place to raise a family," Ginny said. "How can you say such things?"

"Mom," Elias said, a touch of impatience in his voice, "this place was literally founded by adults who disappeared, and to this day people disappear. How can you say it's not cursed?"

"Not to mention all the ghosts and hauntings," Miriam said.

"Does that mean you believe that old wives' tale that Redemption the town, decides who stays and who goes?" I personally wasn't a believer that a town could decide who lives there or doesn't, but I had to admit my own story of how I arrived was a little unbelievable.

"Of course I believe it," Miriam said. "I'm just glad the town let me go."

"It's nonsense," Doug said, rolling his eyes. "I've heard that as well, but I've known plenty of people who have come and gone out of Redemption."

"Or it's possible you were just lucky enough to meet people who Redemption was ready to let go," Pat said.

"That was what I was thinking," Tilde said. "I've had the exact opposite experience, where I've met people who either wanted to move here or wanted to leave and weren't able to."

"What about you, Nancy?" Pat asked, turning to her. "You of all people would know, as most of your customers don't live here."

Nancy eyed Doug, who was still shaking his head in disbelief. "Well, I know it's difficult for people who don't live here to get their head what it's like to live in Redemption. It's not like most places in the world. Typically, people need to experience Redemption for themselves to truly get their head around what it's like to live here. Or, to try and move here and have nothing to work out the way they thought it would."

Very diplomatic, I thought. The group lapsed into another awkward silence.

"What was Ford like?" I asked.

Everyone whipped their head around to stare at me. "Why do you want to know?" Miriam asked, her voice heavy with suspicion.

"Well, I thought you might want to talk about him," I said. "I know he's part of your family, so maybe you want to share some childhood memories or talk about what he was like as a person, so we could all," here I gestured toward Pat and Tilde, "get to know him a bit."

"I haven't seen him in years," Miriam said, her voice cold. "I have no idea what he was like."

"Miriam," Ginny said sharply. "What is it with you? With both of you?" Her glare extended toward Elias. "He was your cousin, and he's dead. I know things weren't always perfect when you were young, and he did get caught up with the wrong crowd, but he was still your cousin, and he did pull himself together. Eventually." She sighed and looked at the ceiling. "What am I going to tell his mother? How can I possibly explain this?"

"I wouldn't know if he pulled himself together or not," Miriam said. "As I said, I haven't seen him in years."

"Neither have I," Elias said.

"Have you spoken to him?" I asked. "Maybe on the phone? Or sent a letter?"

"Nope," Elias said. Miriam also shook her head. I noticed Caleb wasn't responding one way or the other, and in fact, was doing his best not to make eye contact with anyone.

"Hmm," I said. "Why do you think he would show up on your doorstep for Thanksgiving, then?"

"Good question," Miriam said. "I have no idea why he's here."

"Maybe he wanted to connect with his cousins again," Ginny said.

Elias snorted. "That will be the day. But why are you asking us? Maybe you should ask the person who brought him." He turned to look at Caleb.

"Caleb, you brought Ford?" I hadn't realized that was the case, although thinking about it, it made sense. Neither Caleb nor Ford had much contact with their respective families anymore, and it sounded like they had been close when they were growing up, so was it surprising they were still hanging out together?

Caleb was still staring into his wineglass, as if he was hoping if he kept his head down maybe he wouldn't have to talk.

"It was nice Caleb brought Ford," Ginny rushed into the awkward pause. "I was glad to see him. I was glad to see both of them. I thought it would be nice to spend Thanksgiving as a family."

"Sure, Thanksgiving with the family, plus a bunch of extra people," Elias muttered.

I ignored Elias and leaned forward, resting my elbows on my knees. "Caleb, did Ford happen to mention why he wanted to come with you today?"

Finally, Caleb raised his head. I was struck by how dark his eyes were, almost haunted in his face. "He just asked if he could come, and I said sure. I didn't think it was that big of a deal."

"So, he didn't mention why he wanted to come?"

Caleb shrugged. "I assumed it was because he wanted to spend Thanksgiving with family."

It was like pulling teeth. I decided to try a different tack. "How did Ford even know you were spending Thanksgiving with your family? It's not like this is a regular thing."

"I'd like to know the answer to that as well," Elias said, turning to Caleb. "Why did you decide to show up today, after all of this time?"

Caleb stared at me, his expression as still as granite, but his words were directed toward his brother. "As I told you, Elias, I wanted to start building bridges with you and mom and Miriam. We're a family, and it would be nice to act like a family."

"I completely agree," Ginny said. "I would love to have all my children around me during the holidays. It's about time."

Elias coughed. "Bull. I don't believe it for a second. What's the real reason?"

Caleb finally stopped staring at me and turned to his brother. "Why do you think that's not the real reason?"

Elias held his hands out. "Because it's been years and you've shown no inclination to reach out at all. Why would now be any different?"

"People change." Caleb's voice was mild.

Elias scoffed. "No, they don't. They tell themselves they can change, but then they keep doing the same thing over and over again."

"Well, if you don't believe my reason, then why do you think I came back?" Caleb asked.

"That's easy. Because you want something," Elias said, "and if I had to guess, it's money. And no, there's none to be had. My divorce is wiping me out financially. And don't even think about asking Mom. She needs her retirement for herself, not to fund your mistakes."

"I wouldn't think about asking for money," Caleb said, his voice stiff. "I've done quite well, thank you."

"Yeah, I'm sure you have," Elias said.

"I think it's lovely you want to reconnect with your family," I interrupted. As much as I wanted to hear what Caleb had to say while I was able to keep watching the family dynamics, I was starting to think maybe this wasn't going to work, and I was going to have to figure out a way to talk to Caleb alone.

"But I'm curious how Ford would have known this. Are you two friends?"

Caleb stiffened. "I wouldn't call us friends. We do see each other occasionally."

I gave him a surprised look. "Really? Someone you only see occasionally knew you were going home for Thanksgiving? Especially since my understanding is that it was a last-minute decision. Right?"

Caleb's eyes shifted as he looked around the room. "Well, yes, it was last minute," he conceded. "I just happened to see Ford yesterday, and he asked me what my Thanksgiving plans were. I told him, and he said that sounded like fun and could he come, and I said yes." He paused to look at everyone again. "It really wasn't that big of a deal."

"Well, that was convenient," I said. "Seeing Ford the week of Thanksgiving. Especially since you aren't friends or anything."

Caleb stared at me. "I would say it didn't work out very well for Ford, did it?"

I tilted my head. He had a point.

Elias had a disgusted expression on his face. "What crap. Those two have been friends for years. Don't believe a word he says."

Caleb jerked his head toward his brother. For the first time, I saw real anger on his face. "Not everything is what it seems."

"Oh, come on." Elias shook his head with disgust. "Do you really expect any of us to buy this whole 'you weren't friends' act?" He did air quotes around you weren't friends.

"You were never apart," Miriam chimed in. "Wherever Ford was, you were. If you weren't friends, then why did you spend every free moment with him?"

Caleb's face had darkened. "I was young. Things were different back then."

"Yeah, real different," Elias sneered. "You hadn't killed someone back then."

"Elias, that is enough," Ginny snapped. "This is not the time or the place."

"Actually," Wyle said. "I would argue this is the time and place."

Ginny's mouth dropped open, but she quickly recovered. "But why? Why would you possibly want to hear that old news? It's not like it has anything to do with Ford's death."

"Oh, I would say otherwise," Wyle said, but his tone was respectful. "I've often found that during a murder investigation the most unlikely things end up being relevant. So, yes, I think it would be good to hear what happened that day." He paused and gave everyone a pointed look. "Even if it turns out to be not what it seems, or what everyone believes."

"But it wasn't anything," Ginny burst out. "I mean, it was *something*," she quickly amended. "Caleb definitely got … involved with something he never should have." I thought the word involved was an interesting choice, especially if it turned out Caleb had killed a boy. "But it wasn't murder." Her voice was passionate.

"Then where is he?" Elias asked.

"He transferred! That's it. Yes, it was all unfortunate and it would have been better for all if he … if he hadn't felt the need to transfer, but, again, these things happen sometimes —"

Wyle held a hand up, interrupting Ginny. "I would like to hear from Elias, if you wouldn't mind. It seems like he has a … different view of what happened."

"I would say so," Elias said.

"But …" Ginny started to protest but Wyle shot her a look.

"I know this is difficult for you," he said, "and I promise you I'm going to hear all sides of the story, including from Caleb. Okay?"

Ginny seemed to wilt under his gaze, but she nodded.

Wyle turned to Elias. "Tell me what you think happened."

Elias eyed Caleb, who had an unfazed look on his face.

"Go on." Caleb gestured with his hand. "Tell everyone what you think happened."

"I have no idea what happened. All I know is what I saw. Or, in this case, didn't see," Elias said.

"Then tell us that," Wyle said.

Elias looked around the room, the light from the candle casting deep shadows on his face. After all of the bravado he had showed earlier, he seemed oddly reluctant to finally share his story. But then, he took a drink of wine, and that seemed to help, as he straightened his shoulders and started to talk.

Chapter 14

"Everyone called him Willy. That wasn't his real name, but I don't remember what that was anymore. He was ... well, he was one of those kids that was destined to be bullied. Overweight with thick glasses, not great social skills." He looked around the room again, his tone growing defensive. "Not that I'm saying he should have been bullied, but, you know, kids will be kids."

"That's what everyone keeps saying," Caleb said, his voice neutral. "Kids will be kids. Right?

Elias shot him an unreadable look. "You should know."

Caleb held his hands up, palms out. "You're the one who started this game, not me."

"There you go, deflecting again," Elias said, his voice full of disgust.

"I don't understand," I said. "Why should Caleb know?"

Elias's eyes were flinty as he looked at his brother. "Caleb should know because he was one of the bullies. Probably the worst one."

There was a long pause. I looked around the room. Miriam had a bored expression on her face, but I had a feeling she was anything but. Ginny, on the other hand, looked furious.

"Is that true?" I finally asked when it became clear no one else was going to jump in.

Caleb's expression didn't change, remaining as flat as ever. "I'm not proud of some of the things I did in high school, that is true."

Elias rolled his eyes and muttered something under his breath.

"It wasn't just Caleb," Miriam finally spoke. "Ford was part of it, too." She glanced under her eyelashes at her mother, but her mother's expression turned stonier.

I was starting to see the picture. "So, it wasn't just Caleb. Caleb and Ford were bullying Willy."

"And it wasn't just Willy," Miriam said, lifting her head. I could almost see her spine stiffening, even in the dim candlelight. "They bullied lots of kids." She turned to Caleb. "Remember Debbie?"

"Debbie?" Ginny finally burst out. "You're really going to sit there and claim that your brother bullied Debbie?"

"I'm not claiming anything," Miriam said. "All I'm saying is something happened to Debbie."

I held up a hand, feeling like we were getting off course again, and that the whole family needed therapy. Probably a lot of it. "Let's go back to Willy. So Willy was being bullied by Caleb and Ford. Then what happened? Did the bullying go too far one day?

"You could say that," Elias said. "Willy wasn't like other bullied kids. He had a spine. Well, a bit of one, at least. One day he fought back."

I raised my eyebrows. "Really? How did he do that?"

Elias began shifting in his seat, looking uncomfortable. He glanced at his mother, but she refused to meet his gaze. "He accused Ford of plagiarism. Got him kicked out of school."

My eyes widened. I hadn't been expecting that. "He what?"

Elias nodded solemnly. "Ford was pissed, as you can imagine. He was out for blood."

"Well, of course he would be," Ginny said, finally breaking her silence. "He was unfairly accused of a terrible crime."

I held up my hands, giving my head a quick shake. "Wait a minute. Back up here. *Was* Ford plagiarizing? And how did Willy find out?"

Elias looked a little shamefaced. "I don't really know. To be honest, I'm not even a hundred percent sure Willy was the one accusing Ford. But Ford sure believed it."

"He was set up," Ginny said. "The whole thing was dreadful."

My head was spinning. "But you said the school kicked him out, so there must have been some truth to what happened, right? I mean, the school would have investigated."

"Back then, just being accused was enough to get you kicked out. Although …" Ginny paused and looked away. "Ford didn't do himself any favors. He was hanging out with a really bad crowd. Maybe if he hadn't done that, or he wouldn't have gotten expelled."

Miriam looked like she was going to say something, but instead took another sip of wine.

"But I'm still not clear why Willy was blamed for the accusation," I said. "I thought teachers were the ones who caught most of the plagiarism. Right?"

"That's true. It was a teacher who made the accusation," Elias said. "Mr. Shelby. He was the social studies teacher. Not the most aware, if you know what I mean, although that might have been because he was nearing retirement and at that point was going through the motions."

"I don't think he would have noticed if someone had turned in a word-for-word copy of the Gettysburg Address as an original thought," Miriam said.

Elias half-smiled. "Everyone knew if you had him as a teacher, all you had to do was show up regularly in class, keep your mouth shut, and not cause any trouble. If you did all that, it was a guaranteed A or B. The fact that he was the one who somehow noticed the plagiarism was a shock. The rumor was someone tipped him off, because there was no way he would have figured it out on his own."

"But no one is sure it was Willy," I said.

Elias spread his hands out. "It was a long time ago. I don't remember all of these details, but I seem to recall the rumor was someone had seen Willy coming out of Mr. Shelby's office after school one afternoon and the next day was when it all broke."

My mind was still whirling, rearranging pieces in my head. Of all the things I thought Elias would say, I didn't expect this. "Okay, so if I'm understanding this right, Ford may or may not have been plagiarizing, someone accused him, and the word around school was it was Willy. Ford was expelled and … then what? I'm guessing he wanted revenge, right?"

"Oh, yes, he wanted revenge," Elias said, "and boy did he get it."

"But …" my eyes went to Caleb, who was still sitting there, his face emotionless. Why didn't he say something? How could he sit there and let his brother talk about him like he wasn't even in the room. "Caleb wasn't Ford. So, while I guess I can see how this all would have added up to Ford killing Willy, even though that would have been an extreme response, I'm a little unclear why you all think Caleb did it."

"Especially since Willy wasn't even killed," Ginny said.

"Because Caleb did everything Ford wanted," Elias said, ignoring his mother and directing his comments toward Caleb. "Isn't that right? In fact, to this day you're still doing Ford's bidding, aren't you? Even bringing Ford uninvited to a Thanksgiving dinner." His voice was heavy with disgust.

I glanced between them, waiting to see if Caleb was going to answer, but he remained silent. "Bringing someone to a Thanksgiving dinner is a little different than murder."

Elias was still glowering at Caleb. "It still proves Ford had him under his thumb, doesn't it?"

"Maybe, but you still haven't explained why you think Willy is even dead. Your mother doesn't think so."

Elias glanced at his mother, but she didn't return the look. "All I know is Ford had made it clear that he was coming after Willy. The next day, there's no sign of Willy. The principal says Willy transferred, but no one ever saw him again, so no one knows if that was true or not. At the same time, Caleb is also suddenly expelled. You figure it out." He sat back in his chair, crossing his arms across his chest and giving him a defiant look.

I looked at Caleb. "You were expelled? Why?"

"He wasn't expelled," Ginny said. "The principal thought it was better if he stopped coming to school, is all."

I glanced at Pat and saw the same look in her eyes. That sure sounded like the definition of being expelled to me. "Why did the principal think it was better if he didn't come to school?"

"He thought he was a distraction to the other kids," Ginny explained. "With everything that happened with Ford and then Willy he just thought it would be better if Caleb went to a different school. Get a fresh start."

I looked over at Wyle, who had the same skeptical expression I was sure was on my face. "Was that only a suggestion? Could you have told the principal no, that Caleb was staying in school?"

Ginny looked uncomfortable. "Well, it was mostly a suggestion. Although it was also true Caleb had fallen in with the wrong crowd, so that made things more difficult."

"Like Ford had fallen in with the wrong crowd?" I asked.

"Well, they were friends," Ginny said defensively. "I always thought it was nice Caleb and Ford got along so well. I often wished Elias had also hung out with them."

Elias looked at her incredulously. "You wanted me to also hang out with the wrong crowd?"

Ginny looked shocked. "Of course not. I guess I had always hoped that if you had been friends with Caleb and Ford and spent more time with them, you could have kept them from the wrong influences. That's all."

"Oh, so it's *my* fault Caleb and Ford got in trouble," Elias said. "Got it."

"No! That's not what I said," Ginny protested. "I'm trying to give you a compliment, tell you that you would have been a good influence on Caleb and Ford. That's all."

"Caleb, you haven't said much," I interrupted. Man, this was like herding sheep. "This is your life. What do you have to say about what happened to Willy?"

Caleb held his glass up and started twirling it. The red liquid caught the candle flame, transforming it to molten lava in his glass. "What does it matter what I have to say? Elias has it all figured out, don't you?"

"And that's exactly the problem," Elias said, gritting his teeth. "You never once told me what was going on. You never explained what happened."

Caleb continued spinning his glass. "You already made up your mind. What good would it have done for me to say anything?"

"Because I'm your brother," Elias said. He banged his hand against the side table, causing the candle to jump. Luckily, it didn't tip over, although out of the corner of my eye I saw Nancy gasp and press a hand against her chest. "You should have trusted me and told me what happened that night. Why you came home with ..." he suddenly broke off, as if realizing what he was about to say.

No one spoke. I wasn't sure even if anyone was breathing. The silence stretched out for what seemed like hours, but was probably only a couple of minutes. Wyle leaned forward, all his senses alert, the cop firmly in place. The fire crackled merrily in the corner.

"What did Caleb come home with?" I finally said, my voice barely above a whisper.

Elias's eyes darted widely around the room, as if he were a trapped animal. Caleb, oddly enough, looked relaxed, almost peaceful.

"Go on," Caleb said to Elias. "Tell them what you saw."

Elias looked again at her mother, but it was like she had frozen in place, an expression of horror on her face. He dropped his gaze toward the floor and licked his lips. His forehead glistened with sweat in the candlelight.

"That night ..." Elias said, his voice hoarse. "Caleb didn't come home until late, but that wasn't unusual. Caleb didn't come home until late a lot of times back then. It was the middle of the night. Something woke me. I'm not sure what. I decided to go get a drink of water. So I went to the kitchen, which was when I saw the light was on in the bathroom. The door wasn't shut all the way. It was open a crack and I could see Caleb in there. He was standing over the sink scrubbing at something. I went over to see what he was doing, which is when I saw it."

He stopped talking and continued to stare at the floor.

"Saw what?" I asked gently, after a few moments.

It took him a moment to respond, but then he finally took a deep shuddering breath and raised his head. "The blood. I saw the blood on his shirt. He was trying to scrub it off."

For a moment, no one responded. Then Ginny gasped and brought both hands up to her mouth.

"No," she said, shaking her head. "No, that can't be. You're lying."

"I'm not lying," Elias said.

"Or you dreamed it," Ginny said, "or something else happened. It was an innocent accident. Caleb walked into something and cut himself. That was all that happened. Nothing else."

Elias was shaking his head. "Mom, that's not what ..."

But then a loud crash interrupted him.

Chapter 15

Miriam screamed. Or maybe it was Ginny. Or Nancy. Or all three.

"We're all about to be killed!" Ginny had leaped to her feet and was clutching the top of her sweater, one hand shaking.

"I thought you said no one was here?" Miriam demanded. She had sloshed some of her wine on her tailored trousers, but she was too busy yelling at Nancy to notice.

"I don't think anyone is," Nancy said, staring at the ceiling. "Maybe it was a tree branch or something hitting the roof."

"Everyone calm down," Wyle said. He had stood up and was holding his hands out. "Nancy is right. It's probably from the storm."

"That sound didn't come from the outside," Elias said. "That crash came from inside."

"We're going to die!" Ginny said again. "Whoever killed Ford is going to kill us!"

"No one is going to die," Wyle said.

"You don't know that," Ginny yelled. "Tell that to Ford and Tom."

Wyle's expression remained unruffled. "Well, what I do know is panicking never helps. So, let's all take a nice deep breath."

"How can we take a nice, deep breath?" Miriam snapped. She stabbed her finger toward the second floor. "We all heard it. We're not the only ones in here."

"It's possible it's Darla," Nancy mused. "Although I don't remember her knocking anything over before. But there's always a first time for everything."

Ginny grimaced. "Oh, that's right. On top of everything else going on, we also have a murderous ghost on our hands. That's so reassuring."

"Darla isn't murderous," Nancy said. "She's quite sweet. A little feisty from time to time, but she wouldn't hurt anyone."

"Other than the two times where she killed someone," I said.

"Well, yes," Nancy said. "Those were definitely unfortunate incidents."

Now Miriam was on her feet. "Unfortunate incidents? People died and those are unfortunate incidents?"

"The vast majority of the people who have seen Darla were no worse for the wear," Nancy said. "I told you, Darla likes to play pranks every now and then, that's all. And every now and then, it goes a little too far."

"That's it," Ginny said. "You can't possibly expect me to stay in this hotel with a killer ghost."

"I honestly don't think she's intentionally killed anyone," Nancy said.

"She killed Ford!" Ginny exclaimed.

"Well, we don't know that," Nancy said, "especially since I've never seen her use any poison before."

"Enough," Wyle said. His voice, while still calm, had an edge to it. "Let me go check the phones and the weather, but I think we need to come to grips with the fact we're stuck here for a while."

"I can't stay here," Ginny said, wrapping her arms around her. "I'll walk if I have to."

"I'm just going to check the phones again," Wyle said, backing toward the check-in desk. "Stay here."

Ginny watched him go, then shook her head. "This is ridiculous. How can he expect us to stay here with everything that's happened?"

"I told you we should have left hours ago," Miriam said. "Now it's too late."

"It's not too late," Ginny said. "If we want to go, we'll go."

"Mom, I don't think you can leave," Caleb said. "Have you seen how bad it is out there? It's like sheer ice." He waved toward the front door, where the rain and sleet were still slashing against the glass.

Ginny tightened her arms around herself. "I don't care. I can walk home."

"If you try that, you're going to fall and break your hip, or worse," Caleb said. "And did you see how dark it is outside? You really want to be in the middle of all that in the dark?"

Ginny pressed her lips together. "I think I would feel safer out there than in here. At least out there, no one is actively trying to murder me."

"While I'm not ruling out that there's a murderer lurking around in the hotel, I don't know if I would say they're actively trying to murder you," Elias said. "I think you would be dead if that were the case."

Ginny shot her son a look. "How would you know how someone like that thinks? They're crazy."

I waited for Ginny or Miriam, or maybe more likely Elias, to give Caleb the side eye or maybe even a snarky comment about how someone who was able to kill someone would think, but that didn't happen. No one even glanced at Caleb, and I wondered why. Elias had just confessed to literally seeing his brother with blood on his hands, and the rest of the family was oddly uninterested in asking any further questions. I glanced at Pat, then Tilde and Nancy, and could see the same questions in their eyes.

Were they afraid of what the answer would be?

If I hadn't been in the room when the previous crash happened, I would have thought someone in the family had done it, just to stop the conversation from continuing any further.

"Okay," Wyle said, as he returned to the lobby, "the phones are still dead."

Ginny let out a sound that seemed to be a cross between a sigh and a moan.

"So, here's what I think we should do," Wyle said, glancing at her. "Since I know we're all a little on edge, Doug and Caleb and I will go check out the upstairs, and the rest of you should stay down here ..."

Wyle wasn't able to finish as pandemonium broke out. "What? You're going to leave us down here? By ourselves?" Ginny yelled.

"Why are you taking Caleb? You should be taking me," Elias said.

"There's no way you're leaving me alone with these people," Miriam said.

"As owner of the hotel, I really need to be there with you," Nancy said.

"But I want to go exploring, too," Tilde said.

Wyle held his hands out. "Look, it makes no sense for all of us to go tromping upstairs together. Besides, it's safer if you stay in a group."

"But why Caleb?" Elias demanded.

Wyle turned to him. "I wanted to leave you down here to keep an eye on everyone. I wanted at least one man to stay down here."

Elias put his hands on his hips and threw him a steely look. "That doesn't explain why you're choosing Caleb. If he was the one who killed Tom and Ford, he's the last person you should be taking with you."

"Why?" Caleb asked. "Do you think I'm going to jump the police officer the moment I'm alone with him?"

Elias whirled around. "I wouldn't put it past you. Or to hide evidence."

Caleb did a double take. "Hide evidence? How would that work? I haven't even been upstairs."

"We don't know that," Elias said. "When the lights were out, you could have run upstairs."

"Let's do this," I interrupted. "What if I go with Doug and Wyle to search the upstairs, and Caleb can stay down here with Elias and the rest of the group. Would that work?" Even though a part of me wanted to stay with Caleb and Elias and hear the rest of the story, I was also itching to see Tom's room. I was sure there was something we were missing, and even though it might be a long shot, it was worth a look.

Tilde pouted. "Why should you get all the fun? I want to see upstairs, too."

"I wouldn't call it fun," I said quickly, trying to cut off Wyle, who looked like he was ready to nix the idea. "It's more necessary to make sure we're not missing anything. We have to be at the top of our game."

"Oh, for Pete's sake," Miriam said, her voice exasperated. "You're the last person who should be accompanying Wyle. It was your pie which killed Ford and Tom."

"We don't know that yet," I said.

She shot me a disdainful look. "Well, if it was you, talk about getting rid of evidence."

"Which might be a problem if there was any motive for me wanting to kill either Tom or Ford," I retorted. "Considering I didn't even know either of them existed until a few hours ago, it does strain the credibility of why I would want either of them dead."

"Regardless of if you had anything to do with their deaths, it still doesn't make any sense why you should be the one helping Wyle," Elias said. "What makes you more special than anyone else?"

"Charlie has assisted the police on more than one occasion," Pat said. "She knows her way around a police investigation. More than that, she's even solved nearly a dozen cases."

"Well, I helped," I interjected quickly, with a quick peek at Wyle. His expression was impassive, but I knew this would be a sore spot. Not that I was the one who solved the cases, he didn't care who did the actual solving just as long as the right person was caught, but he didn't like amateurs getting involved. According to him, there were too many issues—they could get hurt or screw up the case or something else. But, he did tolerate me, even if he was constantly warning me to be careful.

Pat waved a hand at me. "Oh, you're being too modest," She turned back to Elias. "How many have you been a part of?"

Elias looked nonplussed. "How difficult can it be? Just try not to touch anything, right?"

"Well, it's a little more complicated than that …" Wyle began.

"Oh, for heaven's sake," Elias said. "I know it helps you with job security and all of that, but honestly, how hard can it be?"

Nancy cleared her throat. "Regardless of who else goes with Wyle, I should be there. For legal reasons."

Wyle stared at her. "Legal reasons? What legal reasons?"

Nancy gave him a prim look. "It's my business. I'm legally responsible, right?"

"There's no–" Wyle began.

"I'm coming too," Miriam interrupted. "You're not leaving me alone down here with a killer loose."

"I'm sure that's not the case," Wyle said. "Trust me, it's safer down here."

"You don't know that," Miriam said. "Until you have the killer behind bars, you don't know anything."

Wyle opened his mouth and shut it. I could sense his growing frustration, but he kept his cool.

"And I should come as well," Tilde announced.

Wyle turned to her. "And why is that?" His voice sounded tired.

"Because I might catch something you miss," Tilde said, "and, besides, it sounds like fun."

Wyle closed his eyes. "It's not supposed to be fun."

"Tiki should also come with you," Pat said. Tiki perked up and wagged her tail when she heard her name. "She has a very good nose. She definitely could be an asset."

Wyle's eyes popped open, and he pointed at Tiki. "No. No way. We are absolutely *not* allowing a dog to run loose up there."

Pat sniffed. "I guess I'll just have to carry her then."

"What are we waiting for?" Ginny asked. She was standing up, flashlight in hand. "I, for one, am not going to be able to relax until I know for sure who is in here with us. The sooner we get up there and have a look around, the better I'll feel."

One by one, everyone stood up and collected either a flashlight or a candle. Wyle had a faint scowl on his face, but he didn't say a word and just picked up his flashlight. It seemed he knew he was outnumbered.

"Stay behind me," he said, "and don't touch anything. If I say anything, I expect all of you to listen and do as I say. Otherwise, no one is going up there. Understood?"

All of us nodded. Wyle gave us all another hard look and then strode forward toward the stairs while the rest of us trailed after him. I held back to come up last, after Pat. I wanted to keep an eye on everyone.

Even though I had been up these stairs multiple times, and I had even stayed in this hotel for a couple of weeks when I first came to town, there was something surreal about climbing the stairs in the dark, with only the lights of our flashlight and the one candle Miriam was holding. The pinpoints of lights cast eerie shadows, and the stairs squeaked loudly beneath our feet. A few people muttered something under their breaths as they climbed, but their voices were hushed, as if they too sensed the energy. It almost felt like the hotel itself was watching us, maybe holding its breath as we started our search.

Or maybe it was Darla, the ghost, who was watching us.

"Ouch, you're stepping on me," Miriam said from up ahead. "Watch where you're going."

"Maybe you should move a little faster," Elias grumbled.

"How can I move any faster?" Miriam asked. "Do you want me to shove Tilde aside?"

"Quiet, everyone," Wyle said. "We need to hear what's going on."

Miriam tossed her head but didn't answer.

By the time I reached the top of the stairs, everyone was bunched in the hallway. Nancy was unlocking one of the doors, under Wyle's watchful glare. Most of the hallway remained in darkness, giving the impression we were standing in front of a deep cave.

"Stay here everyone," he commanded after Nancy had unlocked the door. "We're going to search each room one by one. Doug, you and Elias will stand just inside the doorway, and the rest of you stay in the hallway and keep a sharp eye out to see if you see anything strange. I'm going to go in and do the actual searching. Got it?"

"But what if it is Darla?" Tilde asked. "Nancy, didn't you say that Darla attacked men?"

"Darla doesn't attack anyone," Nancy corrected her, "but, yes, she does tend to show herself to men." She paused and tilted her head, studying Wyle. "Actually, specifically men with relationship issues."

I could feel my cheeks grow warm. Next to me, Pat threw me a sideways glance as she hid a smile.

"I'll be fine," Wyle said brusquely. Was his face red as well, or was it just the dim light of the hallway?

"Better safe than sorry," Tilde said briskly. "Maybe you should let someone else do the searching, like Doug or Elias or Caleb."

"You think I want to go in there and face a murderous ghost?" Doug asked.

"Well, we don't know for sure if it's Darla," Tilde said. "We're just being cautious."

"It's bad enough I'm back in Redemption again," Doug said, crossing his arms, "and now to find out I've been staying in a haunted hotel? Forget it."

"Okay, then," Tilde said, turning to Elias and Caleb. "What about you two strapping lads?"

"Hello? I just got divorced," Elias said. "That's pretty much the definition of a man with relationship issues."

"That's true," Tilde mused.

"Why are you asking them, anyway?" Ginny demanded. "If Darla only attacks men, wouldn't it make more sense to send a woman in?"

"Yes, it would, but if it's an actual person, a man would be better suited in that case," Tilde said.

"Actually, a trained policeman would be the best in that case," Wyle said. "Which is me."

"But what if it's Darla?" Tilde asked.

"I'll take my chances," Wyle said tightly.

Nancy clasped her hands together, her brow furrowed. "Tilde has a point. Maybe it should be someone Darla is … comfortable with. Like me."

"You shouldn't be searching these rooms," Wyle said swiftly.

"Darla won't hurt me," Nancy said.

"I'm not worried about Darla," Wyle said, looking like he was trying not to roll his eyes. "I think it would be best if it was me. I've been trained for things like this."

She wrung her hands together. "I know, but … well, no one is staying in this one, so it doesn't matter, but for the ones with guests, I'd rather be the one searching the rooms. It feels less like I'm … well, invading their privacy. They didn't do anything wrong, and here we all are, searching their rooms when they aren't here."

"We're not going through their things," Wyle said. "I'm not interested in their personal belongings. I just want to make sure no one is hiding in their room. If there is someone in the room, I should be the one in front, not you."

Nancy didn't look that reassured. "You're right. I'm just being a silly old woman." She tried to smile. "It's hard to believe something like this has happened in my hotel. Two people dropped dead! During Thanksgiving dinner, no less. I just hope I don't end up losing too much business."

"No one is going to blame you," Tilde said. "I'm sure lots of people die in a hotel every day. And besides, I still think it was an accident. Either Ford or Tom, or maybe both, had a few, well, shall we say *party favors*. It would explain why they had the munchies and decided to eat Charlie's pie before everyone else got a piece."

"I keep telling you, Ford was *not* on drugs," Ginny said. "Tom, on the other hand, is a different story. With his hospital connections, someone really ought to take a closer look at him."

Tilde blinked at her. "His hospital connections? What are you trying to say?"

"Oh, come on, Tilde," Ginny said. "Everyone knows that some of the biggest addicts work at hospitals. All that access to drugs. I bet half of the staff are using on a regular basis."

Tilde put her hand on her hips. "Half the staff? Those drugs are heavily regulated, I'll have you know. I'm not going to say no one is abusing drugs, but to say half the staff ..."

Wyle put a hand on her arm. "Let's focus on the task at hand, and we can talk about it later."

Tilde closed her mouth reluctantly, a grumpy expression on her face.

Wyle disappeared into the hotel room. He was only in there for a few minutes before emerging and, after a quick nod at Nancy, moved to the next room.

"Do you really think we're going to find the killer waiting in one of these rooms?" Pat asked me, her mouth close to my ear.

Nancy was busy unlocking the door, although she seemed to be struggling with it.

"I wonder who would be more shocked," I said. "Wyle or the killer?"

Nancy tugged at the door. Wyle was moving to help her when it suddenly flew open with a bang.

"What the ..." Wyle said.

He never finished the rest of his sentence because he was interrupted by a loud yowl.

Chapter 16

Everyone screamed. Tiki started barking. Wyle staggered backwards, dropping the flashlight. There seemed to be something attached to his chest.

"We're being attacked!" Ginny screeched. "We're all going to die!"

"It's an alien," Miriam said, stumbling to the side and nearly dropping her candle. I heard Nancy gasp, and I wasn't sure if she was reacting to Miriam trying to burn down her hotel or whatever monster had come hurtling out of the room.

Miriam was still shrieking. "I knew I shouldn't have seen that Alien movie. It's coming out of his stomach!"

"Nothing is coming out of my stomach," Wyle said. He had managed to regain his balance and his hands were cupping under whatever it was that attached itself to his chest. "It's a cat."

"A cat?" Nancy took a step forward, adjusting her glasses on her nose. "My goodness, so it is. But where did it come from? No one here had a cat." She peered at the number on the door. "And especially not the Jenkins."

"Why is it all wet?" Tilde asked. She came forward and started petting it. It was hard to get a good look at it, between the uneven lighting and how wet the poor thing was, but it appeared to be a little calico cat.

"Probably because the window is open," Wyle said.

"The window is open?" Nancy looked horrified, and before Wyle could stop her, she ran into the room. "Why, the window *is* open. Why would the Jenkins leave the window open? All the heat is going outside!"

I wound my way through the crowd so I could peer into the room as well. It was poorly lit, even with all the flashlights (and one sputtering candle) but I could see enough that it reminded me of the room I stayed in a few years ago. The hardwood floors were covered with a colorful rug, and a matching cheery quilt was on the queen-sized bed. All the furniture looked like high-end antiques, and were polished until they shone.

The window was open, although not much more than a crack, but obviously enough for a cat to have squeezed its way in. The wind was whipping the curtains around. Nancy slammed the window shut and surveyed the damage.

"Look at this mess. It's soaking wet in here. There's even a puddle."

"It also looks like we found our crash," I said. One of the tables was on the floor, along with a lamp that had broken into a couple of pieces.

"I can't believe this," Nancy said, one hand on her hip. "I'm going to have to have a talk with the Jenkins."

"The room has been cleaned," Wyle said. He had handed the cat off to Tilde, who was cooing over it, and had found his flashlight. He ran the beam slowly around the room. "Unless your guests are in the habit of making their beds."

Nancy frowned and moved to the bathroom. "No, it was definitely cleaned," she said as she came out, a towel in hand, and started mopping up the floor. "I had Jan help me out. She's usually pretty reliable. I can't believe she wouldn't have noticed a window open."

"Maybe the Jenkins came back after the room was cleaned, and that's when they opened the window," Tilde suggested, still petting the cat, who was purring.

Nancy eyed the cat and then went back into the bathroom for another towel, which she wrapped around the cat. "I don't remember seeing them come back, but that doesn't mean they didn't. The last time I saw them was this morning after breakfast. They were heading over to spend the day with their family, but even if they did come back, why on earth would they open the window? Who opens windows in Wisconsin in the middle of November?"

That was a good question, and based on the silence that followed, no one had a good answer. I moved to the window to look out. The rain and sleet were still lashing down, and the trees were tossing and turning in the wind. One tree in particular was close to the building, and the branches scraped against the outside logs. I angled the flashlight so I could see the ground. It was a straight drop to some bushes.

Was it possible there had been a killer in here after all, and he had escaped through the window in the room? I doubted they would have used the tree, because the branches touching the wall seemed too frail to support a full-grown human, although I could certainly see it supporting a small, wet cat. A person would have had to literally jump out the window.

It wasn't a steep drop, just one story, but they would be doing it in miserable weather. It was also impossible to see if the bushes were damaged, like they would have been if they'd broken someone's fall.

And while it was true the window was open, it wasn't open nearly wide enough for a human to get through. That would mean if someone did go out, they would have had to close it once they were outside, but for the life of me, I couldn't see anywhere they would be able to balance themselves while they did it.

Wyle was busy circling the room and checking out all the nooks and crannies, but he had also paused to look over my shoulder and examine the window as well. He didn't say anything, and after a moment, he continued on.

"Okay, so it appears we found our culprit who caused the crash, but I suspect he didn't have anything to do with Tom or Ford," Wyle said.

"If you're talking about the cat, I think she's a she," Tilde said. She had done a pretty decent job drying the cat off and, surprisingly, the cat had let her. In Tilde's arms, the cat looked smaller and more delicate.

"How do you know?" Nancy asked.

"Because she's a little calico, and calicos are always females," Tilde said, holding the cat up. I had to admit, she was awfully cute. "I think she's also hungry."

"We have plenty of turkey," Nancy said.

Tiki let out a friendly little bark and stood up in Pat's arms, wagging her tail. Ever since my big black cat Midnight decided Tiki was acceptable, Tiki had decided she liked cats. The calico cat, however, didn't seem to be nearly as sure of the situation, even though I had a feeling she was bigger than Tiki.

"Anyway," Wyle said, eying the two animals, but both remained in their respective human's arms, "since we're up here, we might as well finish checking all the rooms."

"We might as well," Ginny said. "I know I would feel better if we checked the whole hotel."

"Okay, so let's continue on," Wyle said, with a flourish of his arm.

I started to head toward the door, when I felt Wyle's hand on my arm. "Did you see anything?" he asked, keeping his voice low.

I shook my head. "Although, to be fair, it was so dark it was hard seeing anything. I suppose it's possible the killer managed to find his way into this room and jumped out the window to escape, but that doesn't explain why the window was only open a crack."

Wyle frowned. "Yeah, that was my thought as well."

"Wyle, where are you?" Nancy's voice floated toward us from the hallway. "Are you ready to check the next room?"

"Coming," Wyle said as he hurried out.

I lingered a few minutes, shining my light around the room. There was no reason for it, just a prickling sensation at the back of my neck, like I was missing something, but I wasn't sure what.

As I stepped out of the door, my flashlight beam swept over the floor, and I saw something in the corner. I bent and picked it up. It was a small plastic square with a lid. I opened it and discovered it was one of the traveling pill organizers, the ones that are labeled with the days of the week. It was empty.

I examined it, trying to see if there was a name or a phone number on it, but there was no identification anywhere.

"Charlie?" Pat called out. "Are you coming?"

"Yep," I said, slipping it in my pocket before leaving the room and closing the door behind me. A part of me regretted doing that the moment the door clicked shut. Even though it wasn't technically in the Jenkins' room, it very well could belong to them, and I just took it. Even if it didn't belong to the Jenkins, it didn't mean it had anything to do with Ford or Tom.

But, still, it niggled at me.

***

It didn't take long to search the rest of the rooms, although Doug insisted on being the one to search his own room, with careful supervision from Wyle. I couldn't blame him. I did notice he seemed a little nervous moving around his room, carefully checking all the nooks and crannies that were hiding in the shadows. I wondered if Nancy's talk about the ghostly Darla had freaked him out.

The only room that took a little longer to search was Tom's. Wyle was more thorough, searching the closet, drawers, and the bathroom. I could tell Nancy was uncomfortable watching him go through Tom's personal belongings, but there was no question it needed to be done, and probably wouldn't be the last time his things were searched, and may not be the last time Wyle did the searching. Wyle had also paused from time to time to take a few notes, most likely to share with his fellow officers.

I also wondered what was going to happen with his stuff once the police were done with their investigation. It didn't sound like Tom had much of a family left. Hopefully, he had a will somewhere that would provide some clarity.

"Did you find anything?" Ginny asked as he left.

"Nothing so far, but I didn't search that carefully," Wyle said. "The crime scene team will be more thorough."

Ginny sniffed. "I should hope so. I've heard drug addicts often hide their drugs in places like in the toilet. Can you imagine? You might want to mention to them to check the toilet."

"I'm sure they've got it under control," Wyle said.

"Although it's also possible they won't find any drugs, because he took them all. Probably tricked Ford into taking them as well," Ginny said.

"If there are any drugs involved, we'll definitely get to the bottom of it," Wyle said, ushering everyone into the hallway.

Along with checking all the guest rooms, Wyle checked the storage closets, laundry room, alcoves and more, and found nothing.

"Again, once we can call this in, we'll have the police and crime scene investigators go through the whole hotel more carefully, but I think we can all relax that there isn't anyone else here with us," Wyle said as he led us back to the hotel lobby.

I plucked at Nancy's sleeve to pull her away from the group. "Hey, you got a moment?"

"Sure," Nancy said, looking at me over her glasses that were still perched on her nose. "What did you need?"

I waited until the rest of the group had moved further away from us. "I was curious about Tom. You know him the best, at least of all of us here. Do you think he's a drug addict?"

"No, I don't think Tom was a drug addict." Nancy's voice was firm. "I saw no sign of him doing drugs at all. Sure, he would have a glass of wine or maybe a whisky at night, but that was it."

"But Ginny does have a point that Tom was surrounded by drugs at work," I said. "Is it possible he was stealing drugs? Maybe not to use himself but to sell."

"I don't think so," Nancy said, but her voice didn't sound as sure.

"What is it?" I asked.

She hesitated. "I don't want to speak ill of the dead …"

"Nancy, I think we're beyond that," I said. "Tom is dead, and if we're going to find out what happened to him, we might have to dig through some dirty laundry."

She sighed and looked around, but the group was far enough away they couldn't hear anything. "I know you're right.

It's just … he was really a great guest. Always friendly and ready for a chat. I'm just …" She took a long, shuddering breath, and I realized her eyes were glistening. "This has all been so stressful, so I haven't had a chance to really process that Tom is dead, but it's a terrible shame."

I put my hand on her arm. "I agree. It is horrible. I liked him too, and I just met him tonight. It's very sad."

"And I just … I don't want anyone to get the wrong idea about him."

The back of my neck had started to prickle. "Why would anyone get the wrong idea?"

She hung her head. "This past week, someone was calling and leaving messages. At first it seemed innocuous, but in the past couple of days, they were getting more and more hostile."

"Hostile?" Now she had my full attention. "What do you mean?"

"The man … it was a man … he was getting more and more angry, and he started snapping at me when I asked to take a message."

"Are you sure it was the same man?"

"Positive. He had a very distinctive voice."

"Did you ask Tom about it?"

She raised her head and gave me a horrified look. "No. Of course not. It wasn't any of my business. But …" she paused again. "He did half-apologize for the messages yesterday. Said it was from a previous job. The man had been fired and for some reason was blaming Tom. He didn't get into the details, just said he was handing it and told me he was sorry I had to be subjected to his abuse. I told Tom it wasn't a big deal, it was part of my job, and I hoped he would get it worked out."

My mind was whirling. Was it possible we had gotten this wrong, and the intended victim *was* Tom all along? But if that was the case, how did Ford end up dead? "Do you remember his name? The one calling Tom, I mean."

Nancy straightened up. "Are you kidding? I have copies."

"You have copies of his messages?"

"Yes. I always take messages in a duplicate message book. That way, if the guest loses a message, I can still give them a copy."

"Wyle is going to be thrilled to hear that," I said.

She sagged. "Yes. I'm sure he is." She paused again, biting her lip and looking over toward the group. "And I also don't want Wyle going on a wild goose chase."

"Well, that's part of Wyle's job, to track down leads," I said.

"I know, but …" Nancy scuffed her foot. "Look, I know Ginny wants to believe it's Tom, and if she were to hear this story, she could feel vindicated. Maybe it was drugs, or maybe it was this guy. But, quite honestly, if there were drugs involved, I think it's far more likely they came from Ford and not Tom."

"Why is that?"

Nancy didn't answer for a moment, instead watched the group as they mingled in the lobby. "Look, I know Ginny wants to believe that Ford was a good boy that just fell into a bad crowd, but …

I raised an eyebrow. "But …?"

"I think he's still a part of the bad crowd."

That uneasy sensation prickled at the back of my neck again. "Why do you think that?"

She glanced over toward the group again, and then leaned over to whisper in my ear. I caught a whiff of sage, lemon and rosemary. "He came with Caleb."

I stared at her, the uneasy feeling getting stronger. "You think … it's Caleb?"

"Well, back when they were all in high school, my understanding is Caleb was the instigator. So, if there were drugs involved, and I think there probably were, then it would make sense that they came from Caleb."

"And if they came from Caleb back then …"

Nancy nodded solemnly. "Then he's probably still involved with drugs. Which means Ford is as well. So, if I were to guess, I would say that the drugs came here from Ford and Caleb."

I ran a hand through my hair, feeling more and more sick. If the drugs did come from Caleb, and what Elias just shared about seeing his brother covered in blood all those years ago was true …

Nancy met my eyes, and I could see the same terrible feeling that was lodging in my gut reflected there.

I squared my shoulders. "I think it's time we heard the end of Elias' story."

Chapter 17

"Are the phones working?" Ginny was asking when Nancy and I joined the rest in the lobby. Doug was back at the fireplace, adding more wood, and everyone else had more or less found their way back to their original seats. The darkness seemed even more dense than it had earlier.

"Unfortunately not," Wyle said. "We're just going to have to sit tight a little longer."

"Well, even if the worse does happen, remember, I have plenty of room for everyone to stay the night," Nancy said.

Ginny muttered something under her breath.

"Well, since we're still stuck here," I said brightly, turning to Elias. "Maybe you should finish your story. What did you do after you saw your brother?"

"Why?" Ginny burst out. "Why do we have to keep dredging up the past? Especially when it has nothing to do with anything that happened today?"

"We don't know that," I said. "Since we don't know what happened to Ford and Tom, we don't know what's relevant and what's not."

"Of course it's not relevant," Ginny said. "Tom gave Ford something and ended up killing them both. It has nothing to do with what happened when Ford and Caleb were in high school."

I tilted my head and studied her. "Ginny, one of your sons just confessed to seeing your other son covered with blood the night a fellow high school student went missing and was maybe even killed. Aren't you even a little curious about what happened that night?"

Ginny pressed her hand against her throat as two spots of red appeared high on her cheekbones. "Of course I'm curious," she said, "but this is a family affair. There's no reason to be airing our dirty laundry."

Wyle cleared his throat. "Actually, with all due respect, there's no statute of limitations on murder, so regardless of what happens when we're finally able to investigate Tom and Ford's deaths, I'm still going to have some questions about that night."

"But that's absurd," Ginny said. "I keep telling you, nothing happened to that poor boy. There's nothing to investigate." She turned to Elias. "This is all your fault. Why did you have to bring this unpleasantness up? Isn't it bad enough that Ford is dead? Why do you feel like you have to tarnish his reputation, too? Not to mention drag your brother into this mess."

"Elias didn't do anything," Miriam said. "Ford destroyed his reputation all on his own."

"Miriam!" Ginny's voice was shocked. I was a little shocked as well, especially after what Nancy had said about Caleb being the instigator and Ford the follower. Was that what Miriam meant?

Or was something else going on?

Miriam lifted her chin. "It's true. Ford was awful when we were kids. He did something to Debbie. I don't know what, she never told me all the details, but whatever it was, it was bad ..."

"Stop it," Ginny said. "Right now. I mean it. This is not the time or the place."

"Oh, so you're going to be open to talking about this another time?" Elias asked, his voice bitter. "I've tried to talk to you about this, but you refused to listen."

"Because there's no reason for it ..."

"Oh, so there's no reason to talk about the fact that Caleb killed someone?" Elias asked.

The two bright red spots seemed to become even more red, but the rest of her face was stark white. "We'll discuss it later."

"I'd like to discuss it now," Wyle said, "but I'd especially like to hear from Caleb." He turned in his seat to face Caleb, who was back to playing with his wineglass. "Would you like to tell us what happened that night?"

There was a long moment of silence. It seemed like everyone in the room was holding their breath. Caleb didn't look up, instead he continued studying his wineglass as he spun it in his fingers. He paused for so long, I was starting to think he wasn't going to answer.

Finally, he raised his head, fixing us all with a stare. The candlelight threw shadows against his face, making his skin look gaunt, almost like a skeleton. I shivered despite myself.

"Yes," he said, his voice clear, "I think I would like to tell you what happened that night."

"Caleb, you don't have to–" Ginny began.

"No, I think I do," Caleb said, his voice firm. "It's time. Especially since what Elias said was true." He paused and looked around again. "I did kill Willy."

Chapter 18

No one spoke. No one moved. I'm not even sure anyone breathed. The only sound was the crackling of the fire.

Elias was the first to find his voice. "I knew it." He looked at his brother. "You should have told me the truth."

"I did tell you the truth," Caleb said. "At least, what I thought was true in the moment."

Elias did a double take. "Wait a minute. Are you saying you didn't know you killed him?"

"Not that night, I didn't," Caleb said.

"But this can't be," Ginny said, her voice cracking. "The principal himself told me that boy had transferred to a different school. You couldn't have killed him; he was still alive!"

"I did kill him," Caleb said, his voice eerily calm. "It just took a few years before it actually happened."

"I think you had better start at the beginning," Wyle said.

"I think you're right," Caleb said, putting his wine on the table next to him and settling himself into his chair, as if getting ready for a nice long chat rather than confessing to murdering someone.

"It's all true what you said. I was awful to Willy in high school, and it wasn't just Willy. I was a bully, plain and simple."

Ginny let out a small gasp, and Caleb looked directly at her. "I'm sorry, Mom. You don't deserve to hear any of this, but … well, it's time the truth came out."

"You don't mean it," Ginny said, but she sounded like her heart was breaking. "You were always a good boy. You were so sweet when you were younger. You were the one rescuing the lost and stray animals."

"I know," Caleb said, his voice gentle. "I wish this wasn't the truth."

"But why? Why would you do that? Did you fall in with the wrong crowd?"

"You could say that," Caleb said. He paused and swallowed hard. "It was Ford."

Ginny sucked in her breath, her face confused. "Ford? You mean you fell in with the same bad crowd Ford was in?"

Caleb looked steadily at her. "No. I mean Ford *was* the bad crowd. He was the instigator, not anyone else."

"I knew it," Miriam muttered in the pause. I glanced around and saw that Ginny's face was ashen. Nancy, who was sitting next to her, had a skeptical expression.

"But ... that can't be," Ginny said.

"Ford is ... *was* ... not right," Caleb said flatly. "I'm not a psychologist, but there was something off with him. Power was the only thing he cared about, other than himself, that is. He especially enjoyed controlling people. Making them dance to his little tunes." His mouth twisted in disgust.

"What are you talking about?" Ginny asked. "I never saw that."

"You didn't see it because he didn't want you to," Caleb said.

"That makes no sense," Ginny said. "Why would he want you to see it, and not me?" Ginny asked.

Caleb looked away and, for the first time since he started speaking, he looked uneasy. "Because I was one of the people he controlled."

Elias's mouth flattened in disgust. "Oh, come on. That's ridiculous. How did he control you?"

"I was never good with foreign languages," Caleb said, turning toward his mother. "Do you remember that?"

"Of course I remember," Ginny said, straightening up, a faint glow of pride shining in her eyes. "It was Spanish, and it was such a struggle for you. You had to work so hard, but you did it. Even got a B the last two semesters. I was so proud of you."

Caleb nodded and looked at Wyle. "In order to graduate, we needed to take two years of a foreign language. I chose Spanish, and it was awful. I couldn't get my head around it. In all my other classes, I was getting As with an occasional B, and in Spanish I was in danger of flunking. If I wasn't able to turn it around, I was going to end up in summer school at best and, at worst, I might not be able to graduate. I was feeling desperate. And that's when Ford stepped in and fixed everything."

Ginny looked confused. "Ford never took Spanish. How did he help? Or are you saying he found a tutor for you?"

Caleb stared at his mother for a long moment before answering. "He helped me cheat."

Ginny seemed to not comprehend what her son was telling her. "He did … what? Ford didn't cheat. I don't understand."

"Ford somehow was able to get his hands on all the tests beforehand," Caleb said. "I'm not sure exactly how he did it, but I will say I wasn't the only one he 'helped.'"

"But … that would mean … when he was expelled …" Ginny said, her voice halting.

"That he really was guilty? Yes," Caleb said. "Ford was also very careful. I don't know who turned him in or how they were able to find the proof, but yes. Ford was guilty, and he was furious."

"You don't think it was Willy who turned him in?" Wyle asked.

Caleb shrugged. "I have no idea if it was Willy or not. My role was not to ask questions, but to follow orders. Ford was convinced it was Willy, so Willy needed to be punished." He looked at his mother again. "That was my price, you see. I had to do whatever he wanted. And what he wanted was a front man to take all the blame. So, that's what I did."

"Are you kidding me?" Elias asked, an incredulous look on his face. "This is your defense? You didn't do anything wrong, it was all Ford, but you let everyone think it was you?"

"I didn't say I didn't do anything wrong," Caleb said. "I said my role was to be the front man, which I was. I absolutely did my share of everything I've been accused of: stealing, doing drugs, vandalism." He looked back at his mother. "And bullying."

His mother looked sick. "Oh, Caleb. You should have told me."

"How could I?" Caleb asked. "Ford would have made sure everyone knew I cheated on the Spanish exams. It would have been a nightmare. I would have been kicked out of school, which, of course, happened anyway. But I didn't know it then. I thought if I just did what Ford said for a few years until we graduated from high school, then I would be free of him, but it didn't work out that way."

"If only your father was still around," Ginny said sadly. "Things would have been different. His death changed everything, and I'm so sorry about that."

"What happened with Willy?" Wyle asked, his voice soft and not unsympathetic, but yet trying to keep the conversation on track.

"It was pretty much what Elias said," Caleb answered. "Ford liked to bully Willy. I'm not sure if there was a reason for it, or if it was just Ford liked bullying people and Willy was an easy target. He wasn't the only one Ford liked to torment, but he kept coming back to him over the years. I guess one day Willy decided he had had enough, and somehow found out about the cheating and turned Ford in. Ford was livid. He decided we were going to teach Willy a lesson that day. So, once school was out, we ambushed him."

"Just you and Ford?" Wyle asked.

"No, there were four of us," Caleb said. "Me, Ford, Mel, and Steve. The plan was to grab Willy, take him out to the woods, tie him to a tree, and leave him there for an hour or so. Just to scare him, that was all."

"I take it that wasn't what happened?"

Caleb looked away, a haunted look in his dark eyes. "To this day, I'm not sure if Ford was lying to us from the beginning, or if things just got out of control." His expression was brooding as he continued to stare at the wall, before he finally turned back to Wyle. "We had to tie him up to get him into the back of the van. He fought us, as you can imagine, so it wasn't easy, but there were four of us and one of him, and we were all in much better shape. We took him to this … clearing in the middle of the woods. I don't even know how Ford knew about it. He was directing Steve where to go. After we parked and dragged Willy out there …" Caleb paused again and licked his lips. "Ford decided we needed to strip Willy first, before we tied him to a tree. That was when I first started to get an uneasy feeling about what we were doing, but I went along with it. We took off all his clothes except for his underwear, blindfolded him, and then tied him to the tree. Willy was sobbing by this point, begging us not to do this to him, and Ford started slapping him, telling him to shut up, that he was only getting what he deserved, this is what happened to snitches, and if he didn't shut up, we were going to leave him there all night. He finally quieted down, which was when Ford told us we were leaving.

"Willy, of course, begged us not to leave, but Ford laughed and told him to get comfortable, because he was going to be there all night. Ford wanted to give Willy plenty of time to think about what he had done. As we were leaving, he started to scream. It was …" Caleb shivered. "Blood curdling. I still have nightmares about that scream."

"How long did you leave him?" Wyle asked.

"Longer than I expected. We headed back to the van, all of us trying to block out the screaming. Well, at least Steve, Mel, and I were. I could see in their eyes they were as bothered by this as I was. Ford seemed to revel in it. We got into the van and Ford told us to drive away. Steve protested at that point, saying Willy has had enough and maybe we should let him go. Ford flatly refused, saying we couldn't back down now, and besides, Willy needed to hear the van drive away. Then he would know we were serious. I wasn't sure if he was going to hear the sound of the van, but Ford kept insisting. He finally said if we started the car and drove around the block for ten minutes, we could come back and let Willy go. That was enough for Steve to start the car and drive away.

"As soon as we drove off, Ford said he was starving, and we should get dinner first and then come back for Willy. Hell, we could even bring him something to eat. I wasn't the least bit hungry, but Ford managed to convince Steve to drive to a fast-food restaurant for burgers and fries.

"It was while we were eating when Ford finally let on what his real plan was."

Caleb reached for his wine. I wasn't sure if he was going to drink it or just wanted to hold something. I noticed his hands were trembling and a few drops of wine, now black in the candlelight, had spilled over the side and dripped down the stem.

"I still remember sitting in that car that stunk of greasy food and cigarette smoke. Ford was a smoker. He had also brought a small flask of whiskey that he passed around to all of us. I couldn't eat, but I did take a swig of the whisky, and I still remember how it burned down my throat and into my stomach. To this day I can't stand the smell of fast-food hamburgers, cigarettes or whiskey.

"Anyway, that was when Ford told us we had no choice. We had to leave Willy out there because if we didn't, if we let him go, he was going to go to the police and tell them what we did. Did we really want to go to jail for a stupid fat snitch like Willy? He deserved to be out there. He brought this on himself. It wasn't our fault he had made such poor choices. We were simply reacting to what he did.

"I was horrified. I didn't sign up for this. Mel and Steve also protested, but Ford was very persuasive. He wouldn't stop talking until we finally agreed to leave him out there until morning."

"But why would leaving him out there overnight be better than just leaving him out there for an hour or so?" Wyle asked. "Either way, he would still go to the cops. And arguably, it would be worse for you if you left him out there overnight."

"Ford said we had to scare Willy so badly he would be too terrified to go to the cops," Caleb said. "It didn't make any sense. Even when we were listening to Ford in the van, I think we all knew it didn't make any sense, and I think it was also clear what Ford wanted to do. He wanted to kill Willy, but he didn't want to come out and say that. I think his hope was we would go out there in the morning and find Willy dead, but if that didn't happen, he likely would have found another way to kill him."

"Ford was willing to kill someone because Ford was caught cheating?" Wyle asked.

"It wasn't just getting caught cheating," Caleb said. "It was the loss of reputation. Ford didn't want to be known as a cheater. He wanted to be known as a tough guy. Willy's death was going to send a message to everyone that you don't screw around with Ford."

"So, that's how Willy died?" Elias broke in. "In the middle of the woods?"

"Willy didn't die that night," Caleb said, "and I didn't leave him. After we finished eating, Ford told us we all needed to spend the night at his house. He said it would be easier if we all stayed together until morning. Steve and Mel agreed, but I said I had to go home. I had a paper there I needed for the next day, plus if my mom woke up in the middle of the night and discovered I was gone, she would freak out. He agreed, probably because he never dreamed I would be the one to disobey him.

"But that's exactly what I did. As soon as they dropped me off, I waited until their taillights disappeared into the night, and then I got into my own car and drove out to where Willy was."

Caleb took a long swallow of wine. His hands were still shaking, and a few drops fell on his sweater.

"I found him slumped over against the tree, his skin so pale in the moonlight. I couldn't see him breathe and, at first, I was terrified he was dead. I rushed over to check on him, which is when I discovered he was alive, just in shock. I had a pocketknife, which was good, because I don't think I could have untied him. It still seemed to take forever to saw through the ropes. After I got him freed, I went and collected his clothes for him. Ford had tossed them into the woods. Once he was dressed, I helped him to my car. He was so stiff and sore it was difficult for him to walk. It was clear he didn't want me to touch him, but he also couldn't walk without help. I took him home, and that was the last time I saw him."

Wyle had pulled his notebook out at some point while Caleb was talking and had been jotting down notes. He looked up at that. "He didn't say anything to you?"

Caleb paused and took another swallow of wine. "He only asked me one thing. It was after I pulled into his driveway and before he got out of the car."

"What did he ask you?"

"'Why did you come back?'"

Wyle tilted his head. "What was your answer?"

Caleb smiled, a bitter sort of smile. "I said, 'I don't know.'"

Chapter 19

"So, where did the blood on your clothes come from?" Elias asked.

"When Ford was slapping Willy, he gave him a bloody nose," Caleb said. "I'm guessing at some point while I was either freeing him or helping him to the car is when I got it on me."

"If that's the case, then why didn't you tell me the truth?" Elias asked. "Why did you allow me to think all of these years that you killed him?"

"Don't you get it?" Caleb asked. "I was trying to protect you."

"Me?" Elias was astonished. "How is that protecting me? I thought you killed someone?"

"I knew Ford was going to have his revenge," Caleb said, "and, quite honestly, a part of me thought I deserved it. The last thing I wanted was for him to take it out on the rest of my family, so I kept quiet. I figured if you didn't know, then Ford would have no reason to go after you."

"Did Ford take his revenge?" Wyle asked.

Caleb smiled his bitter smile again. "I was expelled, wasn't I? Ford made sure of that."

"But if you were expelled for cheating in Spanish, why didn't anyone know?" Miriam asked.

"Probably because it was easier to just expel me for being a general troublemaker," Caleb said. "I don't think the principal wanted to do a full-blown investigation, and the cheating had happened in the past. It was less messy this way."

"I still don't understand," Elias said. "Why did you say you killed Willy when you dropped him off at his house? And what happened to him? Why did he never come back to school if what you say is true and you took him home?"

"Would you come back to the same school if you went through what he did?" Caleb asked. "He transferred, exactly like Mom said. To a new school in a different town. Which also explains why no one saw him again."

"Then how did you kill him?" Elias asked.

Caleb paused and looked down into his wineglass. "Willy killed himself."

Ginny gasped. "Oh, no."

"It was while he was in college," Caleb said. "Overdose."

"That's horrible," Miriam said.

"I agree," Wyle said. "I'm so sorry to hear that. Were you in touch with him?"

"No, I found out after the fact. It was ... awful." Caleb's face was blank.

"And you think because Willy killed himself, it was your fault?" Wyle asked.

Caleb let out a bark of laughter that had no humor in it. "I don't see how it couldn't be. Or at least partially my fault. How could it not be?"

"It was a terrible tragedy, but hardly your fault," Ginny said, although she didn't sound nearly as confident as she had before. Her skin had turned gray, and she looked like she had aged twenty years in the last half hour.

"As I said earlier, there's a lot I have to answer for," Caleb said.

"So, I am confused about one thing," Wyle said. "If your relationship with Ford ended after you saved Willy, why did you bring him today?"

"Because it didn't end," Caleb said. "Oh, there was a pause. He was really angry with me, but he eventually came back around. Mostly when my business started to become successful." He gave his brother a sideways glance. "I was wary, of course, but Ford is good. He eventually wore me down and we became ... well, maybe friends is too strong of a word. But we did rebuild some sort of relationship."

"Were you still the front man?" Wyle asked.

"No, nothing like that. He was careful. He never asked me for money or any favors like that. Until yesterday, when he asked me if he could come home with me for Thanksgiving."

"Did he tell you why?" Wyle asked.

"Exactly what I said earlier. About wanting to reconnect with family again."

"Did you believe him?" Wyle asked.

Caleb laughed, an actual laugh. "You know, at first I did. He had been … well, decent for so long, I thought maybe he really had changed. It wasn't until we showed up on your doorstep that I began to get an inkling of what was really going on."

"Which was …" Wyle asked.

Caleb took a long swallow of his wine, nearly finishing it. "As I said, I have a lot to answer for. I've done many terrible things in my life, many things that I'm ashamed of. And the bill just became due."

I shifted in my chair, suddenly very uncomfortable. Ginny squeaked and pressed her hands against her face.

"What do you mean, the bill became due?" Wyle asked gently, since it seemed like the rest of his family had lost their voice.

Caleb took a deep breath and squared his shoulders. "I'm sick. Cancer. The prognosis isn't good."

There was a long moment of silence, broken only by the sounds of Ginny trying to hold back tears as she buried her face in her hands.

"I'm so sorry to hear that," Wyle said, looking uncomfortable.

Caleb inclined his head.

"I'm also sorry that I need to keep asking questions …" Wyle continued.

"It's fine," Caleb said. "I assumed you would."

Wyle looked around the room, his gaze unhappy, but Elias and Miriam seemed to be too shocked to notice, and Ginny was quietly weeping. "Did Ford know?" Wyle asked.

"I didn't think so," Caleb said. "I didn't tell him, but …"

"But?"

"I think he must have found out," Caleb said. "Part of why I'm here is, well, the obvious. I wanted to reconnect with all of you, but, as I said before, my business is successful. Obviously, if I don't beat this diagnosis, it could just be shut down or maybe sold and the money divided amongst all of you. But, if there was a way to bring one of you on board …" He was looking earnestly at his sister and brother, who still seemed to not comprehend what he was saying. "Then I would feel like I had done something worthwhile with my life, that I had created something which would help support someone, maybe all of you, for years. Now, I know this is a lot to digest, and my plan wasn't to get into all of this today, but … well …"

"We understand," Wyle said. "So, how does this relate to Ford?"

Caleb's face went cold. "I think Ford's plan was to get control of my business somehow. I think he came here intending to start the process of building everyone's trust, so he could eventually get his hands on it."

"That's quite an accusation," Wyle said. "Is there a reason why you think that?"

Caleb screwed up his face. "It's hard to explain. There was this moment, right after I parked the car in front of Mom's house. We both sat there for a few seconds, then I turned to him and said 'ready?' And he just … it was almost like a smirk on his face. And he said, 'let the games begin.'" Caleb shook his head. "I know that doesn't sound like much, but his expression, his manner, even his turn of phrase, reminded me of when we were teenagers. For a moment, I almost felt disoriented, like I truly was back in high school and about to do something that Ford was forcing me to do. Then it hit me. This had to be one of Ford's cons. That's how he was making his money, by the way. Running cons.

"The question was, what con was he planning to run on my family? I had no idea. My knee-jerk reaction was to un-invite him, but he was already opening the door and preparing to walk up the driveway, so that was out. The only thing I could have done was to keep quiet and see if I could figure it out before it was too late."

"Why didn't you tell us you were sick?" Ginny burst out. I wasn't sure if she heard a word of what Caleb had just said, but maybe it didn't matter. "We're your family. We would be here for you."

"I know that, Mom," Caleb said. "That's why I'm here now."

With a small sob, Ginny struggled from her seat and ran over to Caleb to wrap her arms around him. Elias and Miriam also joined in, so it was one big group hug.

Without speaking, Pat and I got to our feet in order to give them a private moment. Wyle, Nancy and Tilde had also gotten up, Tilde still holding onto the cat. Doug, however, hadn't moved; he was seated in the corner next to the fireplace, a strange expression on his face, but when he saw us standing up, he also jumped up and followed all of us as we went into the other room.

"That was ... I don't even know," Doug said, rubbing his brow. "I didn't expect that."

"I don't think anyone was," Nancy said, and half-smiled. "I hope you're not too upset you agreed to join us."

Doug smiled back, but it was faint. "It was ... ah ... certainly a Thanksgiving I'll remember."

We were still standing near the door, not wanting to get too close to the table in the middle of the room, as Tom's body was still there.

Doug was patting his shirt and pants pockets, as if he was searching for something. He caught my eye and gave me an embarrassed smile. "Sorry. Such a dreadful habit. Was looking for my cigarettes but, of course, I don't have any because I quit."

"Oh, where are my manners?" Nancy said, her voice strained, like a sad echo of her formerly cheerful self. "Does anyone want anything to eat or drink?"

"Definitely," Doug said. "More wine would be quite welcome. Almost as good as a smoke."

"I suspect you won't be the only one wanting a refill," Tilde said.

"What about you guys?" Nancy asked, turning toward me.

I said I was fine, as I wasn't much of a drinker anyway, and I'd had my limit. Wyle also declined, but Pat looked at us like we were crazy and said she absolutely needed another glass.

Tilde went with Nancy to help, but I think she also wanted to feed the cat more turkey. Doug disappeared to fetch his glass, and Wyle headed over to check the phone again, leaving me alone with Pat.

"What do you think?" she asked, keeping her voice low.

I looked around and took a few steps backwards, so we were closer to the corner of the room. "Well, it sure seems like Caleb had a pretty big motive to kill Ford," I said.

"I was thinking the same thing," Pat said. "If he's dying and he wanted to protect his family from Ford's predatory ways, why wouldn't he?"

"Exactly," I said. "What I don't understand is why tonight?"

"Not to mention, how did he do it," Pat said, "and how did Tom get tangled up in it?"

"Yeah, there are still a lot of questions," I said. All the pieces were whirling around in my head, but I couldn't make heads or tails of them. There was something I was missing. I could feel it. If I could just figure it out, everything would fall into place. I just wasn't sure what I was missing.

Pat was watching me closely. "You've got something, don't you?"

"I don't, actually," I said, "and that's the problem. Where I keep getting stuck is on how it's not clear how Tom and Ford died. It certainly seems like they ate or drank something that killed them, but what? Was it drugs, like Ginny thinks? And if it was drugs, did it come from Tom or from Ford? Either seems likely now."

"An accidental overdose does seem like the most likely scenario," Pat said. "Especially since I don't see how they could have been poisoned and not the rest of us."

"Unless the poison was meant for all of us," I said.

Pat's eyes widened. "What, you think …"

I shrugged. "If the poison was in my pie, then, yeah, it sure seems like it was meant for more than just Tom and Ford."

"But how would it have gotten in your pie?"

"Wyle thought maybe someone broke into my house."

"Are you serious? Someone broke into your house?"

"I didn't see any sign of it," I said quickly. "It's a theory of Wyle's, but if turns out it was the pie, then yeah, he's going to want to search my kitchen."

"I hope Midnight is okay," Pat said.

My stomach lurched. It hadn't occurred to me my cat might get into something he wasn't supposed to. Normally he spent most of his day sleeping in the sun, but, of course, with this storm, there was no sun for him to sleep in. Surely he wouldn't get bored and start nosing around the kitchen cabinets. "I hope so, too."

Pat put a hand on my arm. "I seriously doubt it could be your pie. How could someone break into your kitchen without you knowing it? And how would they know you even were bringing a pie to a Thanksgiving dinner?"

"It does feel like a stretch," I agreed. "More and more it does seem like it must have been something Tom and Ford took by choice."

I saw a light bouncing around a moment before Wyle showed up in the doorway. He took a minute to scan the room before seeing us in the corner and heading over.

"The phones still don't work," I guessed, noticing the grim look on his face.

He shook his head. "I really hope we're not forced to spend the night here. I feel like with everything that's been shared, it would … well, it wouldn't be good."

"Yeah, I agree." I heard a murmur from the other room and realized it was probably Nancy and Tilde refilling wine glasses. "I mean, what a thing to learn, that your long-lost son or brother has cancer and may be dying, but at the same time, we have two dead bodies."

"Not to mention you're surrounded by a bunch of people you barely know," Pat said.

"I feel like that family needs some private time," I said, "but …"

"That's just not practical right now," Wyle said. "Especially since it's very likely someone here is a killer." His voice was flat.

Pat paled at his words. "But that doesn't make any sense. Charlie and I were just talking about that. How could someone have poisoned Tom and Ford without killing the rest of us?"

"I don't know," Wyle said, "and obviously there are a lot of questions we won't have answers to until we're able to properly investigate. Especially with everything that's been revealed tonight, I think the best course of action is to keep both eyes open, and maybe don't eat or drink anything unless it's in an unopen container."

"Including the wine?" Now Pat definitely looked horrified.

"If Nancy opened up a new bottle, you're probably okay," Wyle said gravely.

Nancy was still talking, and I could hear the stress under her words. "Maybe we should go in there now. If we are in danger, we should probably stick together."

"Good idea," Wyle said as we started toward the doorway.

"Besides, I need to ask Nancy if it's a new bottle she opened," Pat said.

As we passed the kitchen, I realized I was thirsty, although I was even less interested in wine after what Wyle had said. "I'll be right back," I said, pushing open the door. "I'm just going to get some water."

Wyle's eyes narrowed. I could tell he didn't like the idea of me going off on my own. "Don't be long."

I stepped into the darkened kitchen, using my flashlight to find a glass in the cupboard, then moving to the sink. As I ran the water and filled the glass, I found myself staring at the dirty dishes, especially the turkey baster and mortal and pestle.

Why had they been moved? Was it just a silly detail that meant nothing?

Or did it mean everything?

The wet glass nearly slipped from my fingers as it hit me. The pieces finally rearranged themselves and fell into place. I couldn't believe I had been so blind.

I finally knew what had happened.

Chapter 20

"There you are, Charlie," Nancy said, still holding the wine bottle. "Are you sure you don't want any? It's a fresh bottle." She wagged it at me.

"I'm fine. Water is great," I said, picking my way across the lobby so I could resume my seat with Pat. I saw that everyone had almost resumed their old seats, except Ginny, who was now sitting next to Caleb, and was holding his hand tightly.

My heart broke a little at that sight. This wasn't going to be easy.

"I can't believe the phones are still not working," Tilde said, as she fed the cat tiny pieces of turkey. Tiki was standing on Pat's lap, watching Tilde's hand as it moved from the turkey to the cat's mouth very closely.

"I know. It's certainly taking longer than I had hoped," Wyle said.

"That's for sure," I said. I crossed my legs and squared my shoulders. "Since we have to sit here anyway, Caleb, would it be okay if I ask you a few more questions?"

"Why?" Ginny asked. "Haven't we gone through enough?"

"It's okay, Mom." Caleb patted her hand before looking up at me. "Sure, what do you want to know?"

"I was just curious how you found out that Willy was dead. Were you keeping track of him or something?"

Ginny opened her mouth, probably to protest again, but Caleb squeezed her arm. "Actually, it was Ford who told me."

I blinked. I wasn't expecting that. "Ford knew?"

Caleb nodded. "Yeah. Apparently, he had run into one of Willy's family members. A cousin, I think, who told him."

"Why would Ford have been hanging around one of Willy's family members?" Elias asked.

Caleb pressed his lips together in a straight line. "I didn't ask, mostly because I didn't want to know. I assumed Ford had searched him out for reasons of his own. Probably to see if he could torment him some more, or just to make sure Willy kept his mouth shut about what happened that night."

"So, you were never contacted by any family members," I said.

"No."

"What about other victims of Ford?" I saw Ginny wince and tried to soften it. "Look, I know this is rough for you, and I'm sorry about that, but based on the fact his dead body is in the next room, I think we need to have this conversation."

"Ford died because Tom gave him drugs. Period," Ginny said. "It's that simple."

"And it might be," I said, "but I think we need to consider the possibility Ford died because of something he did. It's possible he and Tom did take drugs, but the drugs may not have come from Tom. It's possible someone else gave Ford the drugs, maybe earlier this week, and he only decided now to take them."

Caleb cocked his head. "You think someone slipped Ford tainted drugs? It's possible." His voice was thoughtful.

"But I didn't think he took drugs," Ginny said. "At least not anymore."

Elias snorted. "A leopard never changes his spots."

"That's not true," Ginny said. "People stop drinking and taking drugs all the time."

"Ford was drinking tonight, so he was hardly clean and sober," Elias said.

"It's possible Ford was only drinking and not taking drugs," I said.

"Not Ford," Elias said flatly. "He was still the same. You can tell. Even you said he was the same." He waved at his brother. "He might have gotten a little more subtle, but he was the same jerk as he was in high school. He was a con artist, for cripe's sake."

I studied Elias. "You seem pretty convinced he was taking drugs."

Elias stared back at me, his eyes lidded. "I know my cousin."

"I'm sure you do." I leaned forward. "Is there another reason why you would think Ford was on drugs?"

Elias looked at me suspiciously. "What are you suggesting?"

"I'm suggesting that maybe *you* offered him drugs."

Elias's mouth dropped open. "Why would I have drugs? I don't take drugs."

"How about any other drugs? I mean prescription drugs, nothing illegal."

Elias' mouth snapped shut and he straightened up. "I don't see what business that is of yours. I don't like your tone or what you're implying."

"I'm just looking at all the angles," I said. "You've made your disgust of Ford clear, so is it so far out of bounds to think you might have slipped something to him?"

Elias's eyes blazed at me. "Yes, in fact, it *is* out of bounds. He's still my cousin, no matter what happened. Besides, I'm not a killer."

"What about you, Miriam?" I asked, turning to her.

Miriam's face closed down. "What about me?"

"Are you taking any prescription drugs?"

"I didn't kill Ford, if that's what you're implying," Miriam said archly.

"Well, someone did," I said, "and, unfortunately all three of you have a motive. At least for Ford, Tom not so much."

"This is ridiculous," Miriam said. "I may not have cared for Ford, but I certainly had no reason to kill him."

"Other than he might have done something to your friend back in high school," I said, "and who knows what else he did."

Miriam gritted her teeth. "I didn't kill him."

"What's wrong with you?" Ginny asked. "Why are you attacking my family?"

"I'm not attacking anyone," I said. "I'm just asking questions. I know the timing isn't great, but we have to get to the bottom of what's going on." I glanced over toward Doug. "How about you, Doug? Do you take any prescription medicine?"

Doug's mouth was a perfect O. "Uh … I … Why are you asking me?" He stuttered. "I had no reason to kill Ford."

"I didn't say you did," I said, "but knowing if you are taking any prescription drugs would be helpful."

"I …" His eyes darted around the room, and he licked his lips, "I don't think it's any of your business."

"It probably isn't," I agreed, "but it might still be helpful, as I think I have figured out how Tom and Ford were killed."

"You have?" Wyle asked in surprise. Actually, everyone was staring at me with various forms of astonishment on their faces.

"Yes, I think what happened is someone added drugs to my pie. They used the mortar and pestle to grind up the pills, dissolved them in water, and injected them into the pie."

"How did you figure that out?" Wyle asked.

"If you look closely, you can see little holes in the pie." That was a complete lie, but I wanted to see the expressions on everyone's faces. I pulled the little travel pill case out of my pocket. "Oh, and I found this, too. Upstairs by one of rooms."

"You found that upstairs?" Nancy asked. "You took that out of one of the rooms?"

"No, I found it in *front* of one of the rooms." I looked around again. "Like maybe someone had tossed it there, hoping it would seem like it was left by a guest."

"But you don't think it was?" Nancy asked.

"It's kind of hard to miss," I said. "It was right there in the hallway. You were up there cleaning earlier. Did you see it then?"

She shook her head slowly, still staring at it.

"Does this look familiar to anyone?" I asked, shaking the pill container as I held it up. I continued to watch everyone's faces very carefully. Everyone was staring at me in bewilderment or wonderment, except …

"Doug, you had said earlier this is your first time in Redemption. Is that right?" I asked.

Doug gave me a double take. "Wh … what does that have to do with anything?"

"Probably nothing," I said, "but if it turns out you were on some sort of prescription drugs, maybe even the same prescription drugs that killed Tom and Ford, the fact you never met either of them until recently would probably mean that it was just a big coincidence. Right?"

Doug's body seemed to relax. "Oh, right. Yes. It's my first time in Redemption."

I nodded. "That's what I thought. Except …" I tapped my finger against my lips, "you had said when you were first introduced that it *wasn't* your first time in Redemption. You had to 'come back,' if I'm recalling correctly. So … which is it?"

Doug blinked owlishly at me. "I'm … I don't know what you're talking about."

I smiled sweetly. "Oh, I think you do. In fact," I lowered my voice to an almost confidential tone, "I think you knew exactly who Ford is."

Doug looked at me in horror. "No … I … No, I told you, I've never seen him before."

"Actually, I think you have," I said. "I think either you or someone in your family was one of Ford's victims. Isn't that right?"

"I … I don't know what you're talking about," Doug said faintly. All the blood had left his face, leaving him as pale as a ghost.

"It must have been quite a shock to see him, wasn't it?" I continued. "But maybe the bigger shock was how he didn't recognize you. Was that when the seed was planted that maybe this was your chance for revenge? After all these years?"

"No! That's not true. I'm not a murderer," Doug said.

I raised my eyebrows. "Oh? Was his death an accident, then?"

"Wait a minute," Caleb said suddenly. He had been studying Doug. "Do I know you?"

"No, I've never met any of you," Doug said as he pressed himself backwards in his chair, as if he were trying to disappear into the shadows.

Caleb was tapping his chin. "No, I'm sure I have."

Suddenly, Elias blanched. "It can't be."

Doug froze.

Caleb glanced at his brother. "What?"

"I see it, too," Miriam said, a horrified expression on her face. "You're related to Willy, aren't you?"

Doug opened his mouth to protest, but no sound came out.

"You're right," Caleb said, squinting at him. "You do look like Willy." He cocked his head as he kept studying him. "You must be the cousin. The one who told Ford what happened to Willy." His expression became sad. "I'm so very sorry. I know there's nothing I can say that will make it better, but I truly am sorry."

The change happened so fast it nearly took my breath away. One moment, Doug was so pale he looked like he was turning into a corpse, and then the next moment, his expression was suddenly consumed with rage. "You're sorry? You think that's going to change anything?"

Caleb blinked. "No, no, of course not …"

"You think you sitting around talking about how bad you feel because you killed Willy is going to change anything? Oh, boo hoo hoo, you feel so guilty now. Too bad! Do you have any idea the pain you caused? Not even that night, but the *years* of bullying. You think one apology can make up for that?"

"Oh, my gosh," Caleb said. Now he was as pale as Doug was a moment ago. "You're not related to Willy. You *are* Willy. You didn't die after all."

"No, you're wrong about that," Doug said. "Willy *did* die. Over and over and over, until one day he tried to make it official. He was in hell anyway, never very far from the nightmares. So, what was the point of all that suffering? At least if he was dead, he would hopefully be at peace."

"So, what happened?" I asked quietly.

Doug did a double take, as if it suddenly occurred to him what he had been saying. His eyes were round as his gaze darted around the room, as if he were searching for a way to escape.

"We're going to find out the truth," Wyle said. "You know that. Wouldn't you rather it came from you?"

Doug didn't answer, instead eying the front door, as if trying to determine if he could run out of the hotel before Wyle caught him. He must have decided Wyle was in a little better shape than he was, because he finally turned back toward us, squaring his shoulders and taking a deep breath. "It's true. My given name was William. My middle name was Douglas. When I woke up in the hospital after my overdose, at first I was furious. I couldn't believe I was still alive. Was I so much of a screwup I couldn't even kill myself without messing it up?

"But, eventually, I came to see that this was a chance for a fresh start. Even if my body didn't die, it didn't mean I couldn't kill William off. This was my chance to start over and build a new life. I could become someone who had never been bullied, who hadn't been stripped and left tied up and blindfolded in the middle of the woods one night.

"I changed my name legally, not just my first name, but my last name as well. I used my mother's maiden name. I was hoping that would be the olive branch that I meant it to be, but ... well, my family didn't agree with what I was doing at all. They thought I should be getting therapy, not changing my name, losing weight, changing my appearance with a nose job, and moving to a different city. We fought about it. A lot. Eventually it just seemed easier to not see them anymore. I even convinced myself it was for the best. Not having anyone around me who knew of Will's history would make it easier for me to become Doug."

"Did it work?" I asked, my voice gentle. Despite the fact this man had killed not one but two people, and one of those people had never done anything to him, I couldn't help but feel a little sorry for him.

Doug's lips twisted in a grimace. "Almost. I would be fine for days, weeks, months. Then, suddenly, I would be hit by terrible anxiety attacks or awful depression. Some of those episodes were so bad I couldn't get myself out of bed. Work suffered. Finally, I was told if I didn't get myself under control, I was going to lose my job, so I made an appointment to see a psychiatrist, but not for therapy. For pills. And they worked. While I still suffered occasionally from anxiety or depression, it wasn't so bad I couldn't work. I thought I had cured it.

"Then, my company decided that Redemption would be a great place for a new treatment center. I tried to talk them out of it, but I was overruled. That was okay, I told myself. Just because there was a treatment center here didn't mean I would ever have to come back to Redemption.

"But then the person who was supposed to be in the point position for this project had to quit unexpectedly. Her mother was doing poorly and she had to drop everything and move to Colorado to take care of her. And, just like that, I became the point person. And, just like that, I was having to travel to Redemption.

"So, I did what any normal person would do. I went back to my doctor and had him up my prescription. I told myself I would be okay. It would only be a few weeks. And I decided if I worked over the Thanksgiving holiday and didn't come back and forth, I could make my time there even shorter. It was going to be fine. And, for a while, it seemed like it was going to be fine. Until …" he broke off and stared at the wall, a brooding expression on his face.

"Until Ford walked into your Thanksgiving celebration," I said.

Doug snapped his head toward me, a snarl on his face. "Not just Ford. Caleb, too."

Caleb blanched. Next to him, Ginny gasped and squeezed his hand even harder.

"And when they didn't recognize you, you decided to get your revenge," I said.

Doug almost smiled. "I couldn't believe my luck. When I first saw them, it was all I could do to not race back to my room. But, then when I realized they had no idea who I was, I thought maybe I could have some fun. It wasn't until I was watching how much everyone was drinking that I got the idea to add a little … extra something to the wine."

"Your medication you mean," I said.

"I didn't think it would kill them," Doug said. "I wasn't trying to kill anyone. I figured the worst that would happen is they would get sick. Miserably sick. Hopefully, it would last a few days. I would have preferred it to have lasted as long as it took me to recover from being left in the woods, but hey, beggars can't be choosers."

"But you didn't spike their drinks, did you?" I asked. "You spiked the pie."

"It was when the lights went out," Doug said. "I realized that was my chance. I could go in and spike the wine. Except when I went into the kitchen, I didn't see any open wine bottles. What was I going to do? Then, I saw the pies and remembered Ford taking about how he couldn't wait to try the mincemeat pie. And then I saw the mortar and pestle and turkey baster sitting near the sink, and it was like fate or something. Like following a trail of breadcrumbs. I couldn't believe how easy it was."

"But … we all were going to eat the pie," Tilde said. "You were going to kill all of us."

"As I said, I didn't think I was going to kill anyone," Doug said. "But also, why do you think I ran into the kitchen to pass out pieces of pie? I was going to just give a piece to Caleb and Ford, and 'accidentally' have the rest of the pie end up on the floor. I'm not a monster." He looked wildly around at all of us. "I'm not! It's not my fault Tom was snacking on pie before dessert was served. How could I have known he was going to cheat and eat pie before the meal? It wasn't my fault!"

The silence that answered him was deafening.

Chapter 21

"Next year for Thanksgiving, I think we should just stay home and eat dessert," Pat said. We were sitting in my warm cozy kitchen, the winter sun shining through the windows, with tea and big pieces of freshly baked lemon pie in front of us. Midnight was snoozing in the sun and Tiki was on Pat's lap, keeping a sharp eye on Pat as she ate her pie. "That way, we don't have to worry about any baked goods being poisoned."

"Sold," I said, toasting her with my teacup.

Once Doug had confessed, everything shifted, almost like someone or something had been keeping us in a strange little bubble until we were finally able to crack the case. Pat thought it was Redemption's doing, but I was more inclined to think it was Darla. Nancy had made an offhand comment that she thought Darla had liked Tom, and I wondered if maybe this was her way of getting justice for him.

But, whatever it was, the next time Wyle checked the phones, they were working.

The investigation proved exactly what Doug had confessed to: Tom and Ford had died from an overdose-sized cocktail of antidepressants mixed with alcohol. As it turned out, Doug was on quite a few prescriptions. The mincemeat pie was full of injected drugs, so much it was impossible to think Doug was just trying to make them sick, but he continued to insist it was all a terrible accident. According to him it had been dark in the kitchen, he had no idea of the dosage, nor how much they would eat.

It was possible he truly believed he didn't want to kill anyone, but I suspected his subconscious had different ideas.

Once they were both dead, my guess is that Doug panicked, which is why he dropped his traveling pill case in front of the hotel room. Maybe he was hoping the police would assume whoever opened the window had dropped the case, but, of course, that didn't happen.

And then there was the matter of the window being open, which was still a mystery. The Jenkins were adamant they hadn't touched the window, and Jan swore it had been closed when she cleaned the room. It was all very puzzling.

"Maybe Darla opened it," Pat had suggested.

"Darla can't open up windows," Nancy said, but her voice was hesitant, as if she was considering it. "Besides, why she would do such a thing?"

"Maybe to help out Sherlock," Tilde said. Tilde had ended up adopting the little calico cat, as no one had claimed her. She was now named Sherlock, despite Pat telling her that was a silly name for a female cat. Tilde said she didn't care.

"She's going to be the new mascot at the Redemption Detective Agency," Tilde said proudly. Pat just rolled her eyes.

"As much fun as it is to solve mysteries," Pat said, forking up a big bite of lemon pie, "and as much as I love a good Thanksgiving meal, I think I'd prefer to skip the part where we're trapped in a hotel with no electricity or phones and a killer on the loose."

She had a point, although it was still difficult for me to think of Doug in those terms. Even though he did kill two people, a part of me still felt sorry for the teenager who was so badly bullied. Not that it made what he did right, but it was still sad.

"It wasn't all bad," I said. "It seems that Ginny and her three kids have made a fresh start at being a family again."

"That's true," Pat said. "And it also sounds like both Miriam and Elias are going to help run Caleb's business. So, that's good. I hope it works out."

"So do I," I said, my thoughts drifting back to my own strained family relations. Maybe I should give my sister, Annabelle, a call today.

"But all that said," Pat said, slipping Tiki a piece of crust, "I still feel cheated. We got no pie this year for Thanksgiving. That is a complete travesty."

"So, I guess that means next year, we're only eating pie and nothing else," I said.

Pat held up her fork. "Now you're talking."

A Word From Michele

Can't get enough of Charlie? I've got you covered. Keep going with *A Room for Murder,* a Charlie Kingsley cozy novella and her very first case, now available on preorder.

Preorder your copy right here:

https://MPWNovels.com/r/bcornroomamzn

***

You can also check out exclusive bonus content for *A Cornucopia of Murder,* along with the other Charlie Kingsley books.

The bonus content reveals hints, clues, and sneak peeks you won't get just by reading the books, so you'll definitely want to check it out. You're going to discover a side of Redemption that is only available here:

MPWNovels.com/r/corn-bonus

***

If you enjoyed *A Cornucopia of Murder*, it would be wonderful if you would take a few minutes to leave a review and rating on Amazon:
www.amazon.com/dp/B0BFC7MN2G#customerReviews
Goodreads:
goodreads.com/book/show/199912957-a-cornucopia-of-murder
or Bookbub:
www.bookbub.com/books/a-cornucopia-of-murder-charlie-kingsley-mysteries-book-7-by-michele-pariza-wacek

(Feel free to follow me on any of those platforms as well.) I thank you and other readers will thank you (as your reviews will help other readers find my books.)

The *Charlie Kingsley Mysteries* series is a spin-off from my award-winning *Secrets of Redemption* series. *Secrets of Re-*

demption is a little different from the *Charlie Kingsley Mysteries*, as it's more psychological suspense, but it's still clean like a cozy.

You can learn more about both series, including how they fit together, at MPWNovels.com, along with lots of other fun things such as short stories, deleted scenes, giveaways, recipes, puzzles and more.

I've also included a sneak peek of the first book in the Secrets of Redemption series, *It Began With a Lie*, just turn the page to get started.

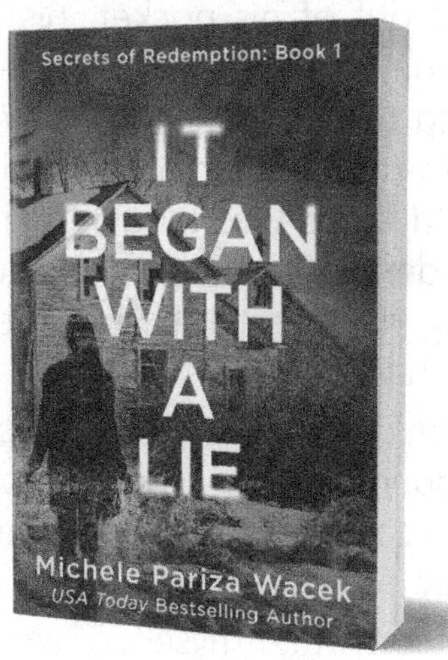

It Began With a Lie - Chapter 1

"You're right. It's perfect for us. I'm so glad we're here," I said, lying through my carefully pasted-on smile.

I tried to make my voice bright and cheery, but it sounded brittle and forced, even to me. I sucked in my breath and widened my smile, though my teeth were so clenched, my jaw hurt.

Stefan smiled back—actually, his mouth smiled but his dark-brown eyes, framed with those long, thick lashes any woman would envy, looked flat … distracted. He hugged me with one arm. "I told you everything would be okay," he whispered into my hair. His scent was even more musky than usual, probably from two straight days of driving and lack of shower.

I hugged him back, reminding myself to relax. *Yes, everything is going to be okay. Remember, this move represents a fresh start for us—time for us to reconnect and get our marriage back on track. It's not going to happen overnight.*

His iPhone buzzed. He didn't look at me as he dropped his arm and pulled it out of his pocket, his attention already elsewhere. "Sorry babe, gotta take this." He turned his back to me as he answered the call, walking away quickly. His dark hair, streaked with silver that added a quiet, distinguished air to his All-American good looks was longer than normal, curling around his collar. He definitely needed a haircut, but of course, we couldn't afford his normal stylist, and not just anyone was qualified to touch his hair.

I wrapped my arms around myself, goosebumps forming on my skin as a sudden breeze, especially cool for mid-May, brushed past me—the cold all the more shocking in the absence of Stefan's warm body.

He has to work, I reminded myself. *Remember why we're here.*

I remembered, all right. How could I forget?

I rubbed my hands up and down my arms as I took a deep breath, and finally focused on the house.

It was just as I remembered from my childhood—white with black shutters, outlined by bushy green shrubs, framed by tall, gently-swaying pine trees and the red porch with the swinging chair. It sat all by its lonesome in the middle of a never-developed cul-de-sac, the only "neighbors" being an overgrown forest on one side, and a marshy field on the other.

Okay, maybe it wasn't *exactly* the way I remembered it. The bushes actually looked pretty straggly. The lawn was overgrown, full of dandelions going to seed, and the porch could definitely use a new paint job.

I sighed. If the outside looked like this, what on earth waited for me on the inside?

Inside.

I swallowed back the bile that rose in the back of my throat. It slid to my stomach, turning into a cold, slimy lump.

The house of my childhood.

The house of my nightmares.

Oh God, I so didn't want to be here.

Stefan was still on the phone, facing away from me. I stared longingly at his back. *Turn around*, I silently begged. T*urn around and smile at me. A real smile. Like how you used to before we were married. Tell me it's going to be okay. You don't have to leave tonight like you thought. You realize how cruel it would be to leave me alone in this house the first night we're here, and you don't want to do that to me. Please, tell me. Or, better yet, tell me we're packing up and going back to New York. Say this was all a mistake; the firm is doing fine. Or, if you can't say that, say we'll figure it out. We'll make it work. We don't need to live here after all. Please, Stefan. Please don't leave me alone here.*

He half-turned, caught my eye, and made a gesture that indicated he was going to be awhile.

And I should start unpacking.

I closed my eyes. Depression settled around me like an old, familiar shawl. I could feel the beginning of a headache stab my temples.

Great. Just what I needed to complete this nightmare—a monster headache.

I turned to the car and saw Chrissy still in the backseat—headset on, bobbing to music only she could hear. Her long, dark hair—so dark it often looked black—spread out like a shiny cloak, the ends on one side dyed an electric blue.

Oh, yeah. That's right. I wouldn't be alone in the house after all.

Chrissy closed her eyes and turned her head away from me.

It just kept getting better and better.

I knocked on the window. She ignored me. I knocked again. She continued to ignore me.

For a moment, I imagined yanking the door open, snatching the headset off and telling her to—no, *insisting* that—she get her butt out of the car and help me unpack. I pictured her dark brown eyes, so much like Stefan's, widening, her pink lip-glossed mouth forming a perfect O, so shocked that she doesn't talk back, but instead meekly does what she's told.

More pain stabbed my temples. I closed my eyes and kept knocking on the window.

It's not her fault, I told myself for maybe the 200th time. *How would you act if you were sixteen years old and your mother abandoned you, dumped you at your father's, so she'd be free to travel across Europe with her boy toy?*

I squelched the little voice that reminded me I wasn't a whole heck of a lot older than said boy toy, and started pounding on the window. Stefan kept telling me she was warming up to me—I personally hadn't seen much evidence of that.

Chrissy finally turned her head and looked at me. "What?" she mouthed, disgust radiating off her, her eyes narrowing like an angry cat.

I motioned to the trunk. "I need your help."

Her lip curled as her head fell back on to the seat. She closed her eyes.

I had just been dismissed.

Great. Just great.

I looked around for Stefan—if he were standing with me, she would be out of the car and helping—a fake, sweet smile on her face, but he had moved to the corner of the street, still on the phone. I popped the trunk and headed over to him. Maybe I could finally get him to see reason—that it really was a dreadful idea to leave the two of us alone in Redemption, Wisconsin, while he commuted back and forth to New York to rescue his failing law firm. "See," I could say, "She doesn't listen to me. She doesn't respect me. She needs her father. I need you, too. She's going to run wild with you gone and I won't be able to deal with her."

Stefan hung up as I approached. "The movers should be here soon. You probably should start unpacking." Although his tone was mild, I could still hear the underlying faint chords of reproach—what's going on with you? Why haven't you started yet? Do I need to do everything around here?

"Yes, I was going to," I said, hating my defensive tone, but unable to stop it. "But there's a problem I think you need to deal with."

His eyes narrowed—clearly, he was losing his patience with me. "What?"

I opened my mouth to tell him about Chrissy, just as her voice floated toward us, "Can I get some help over here?"

I slowly turned around, gritting my teeth, trying not to show it. Chrissy stood by the trunk, arms loaded with boxes, an expectant look on her face. The pain darting through my head intensified.

"Rebecca, are you coming?" Stefan asked as he headed over to his charming daughter, waiting for him with a smug expression on her face, like a cat who ate the canary. I took a deep breath and trudged over, the sick knot in the pit of my stomach growing and tightening.

What on earth was I going to do with her while Stefan was gone?

Chrissy threw me a triumphant smile as she followed her father to the house. I resisted the urge to stick my tongue out at her, as I heaved a couple of boxes out of the trunk.

Really, all the crap with Chrissy was the least of my worries. It was more of a distraction, than anything.

The real problem was the house.

The house.

Oh God.

I turned to stare at it. It didn't look menacing or evil. It looked like a normal, everyday house.

Well, a normal, everyday house with peeling paint, a broken gutter and a few missing roof shingles.

Great. That probably meant we needed a new roof. New roofs were expensive. People who had to rescue failing law firms tended to not have money for things like new roofs. Even new roofs for houses that were going to be fixed up and eventually sold, ideally for a big, fat profit.

Would there be *any* good news today?

Again, I realized I was distracting myself. New roofs and paint jobs—those were trivial.

The real problem was *inside* the house.

Where all my nightmares took place.

Where my breakdown happened.

Where I almost died.

I swallowed hard. The sun went behind a cloud and, all of a sudden, the house was plunged into darkness. It loomed in front me, huge and monstrous, the windows dark, bottomless eyes staring at me … the door a mouth with sharp teeth …

"Rebecca! Are you coming?"

Stefan broke the spell. I blinked my eyes and tried to get myself together.

I was being silly. It was just a house, not a monster. How could a house even BE a monster? Only people could be monsters, which would mean my aunt, who had owned the house, was the monster.

And my aunt was dead now. Ding, dong, the witch is dead. Or, in this case, the monster.

Which meant there was nothing to fear in the house anymore. Which was exactly what Stefan kept telling me back in New York, over and over.

"Don't you think it's time you put all this childhood nonsense behind you?" he asked. "Look, I get it. Your aunt must have done something so dreadful that you've blocked it out, but she's dead. She can't hurt you anymore. And it couldn't have worked out any more perfectly for us—we have both a place to live rent-free right now, while I get things turned around. And, once we sell it, we can use the money to move back here and get a fresh start."

He was right, of course. But, still, I couldn't drop it.

"Why did she even will the house to me in the first place?" I persisted. "Why didn't she will it to CB? He was there a lot more than I was."

Stefan shrugged. "Maybe it was her way of apologizing to you all these years later. She was trying to make it up to you. Or maybe she changed—people said she was sick at the end. But, why does it matter why she willed it to you? The point is she did, and we really need it. Not to mention this could be a great way for you to finally get over whatever happened to you years ago."

Maybe. Back in New York, it had seemed so reasonable. So logical. Maybe the move wouldn't be a problem after all.

But, standing in the front yard with my arms filled with boxes, every cell in my body screamed that it was a really awful idea.

"Hey," Stefan whispered in my ear, his five o'clock shadow scratching my cheek. I jumped, so transfixed by the house that I hadn't even realized he had returned to me. "Look, I'm sorry. I should have known this would be rough for you. Come on, I'll walk in with you."

He rubbed my arm and smiled at me—a real smile. I could feel my insides start to thaw as all those old, exciting, passionate feelings reminiscent of when we first started dating swarmed over me. I remembered how he would shower me with red roses and whisk me off to romantic dinners that led to steaming, hot sex. He made me feel like a princess in a fairy tale. I still couldn't fathom how he ended up with me.

I met his eyes, and for the first time in what seemed like a long time, I felt the beginnings of a real smile on my lips. *See, he does care, even if he doesn't always show it. This is why the move was the perfect thing for our marriage; all we needed was to get away from the stress of New York, so we could rekindle things.* I nodded and started walking with him toward the house. Over her shoulder, Chrissy shot me a dirty look.

The closer we got to the house, the more I focused on my breathing. *It's going to be okay, I repeated to myself. It's just a house. A house can't hurt anyone. It's all going to be okay.*

An owl hooted, and I jumped. Why was an owl hooting in the daytime? Didn't that mean someone was going to die? Isn't that what the old stories and folklore taught? My entire body stiffened—all I wanted to do was run the other way. Stefan hugged me closer, gently massaging my arm, and urged me forward.

"It's going to be okay," he murmured into my hair. I closed my eyes for a moment, willing myself to believe it.

We stepped onto the porch, Chrissy impatiently waiting for Stefan to unlock the door. He put the boxes on the ground to fumble for his keys as I tried hard not to hyperventilate.

It's just a house. A house can't hurt anyone.

After an eternity that simultaneously wasn't nearly long enough, he located the keys and wrenched the door open, swearing under his breath.

His words barely registered. I found myself compelled forward, drawn in like those pathetic moths to the killing flame.

I could almost hear my aunt excitedly calling, "Becca? Is that you? Wait until you see this," as I stepped across the threshold into the house.

It was exactly like I remembered.

Well, maybe not exactly—it was filthy and dusty, full of cobwebs and brittle, dead bugs lying upside down on the floor with their legs sticking up. But I remembered it all—from the overstuffed floral sofa where I spent hours reading, to the end table covered with knick-knacks and frilly doilies, to the paintings lining the walls. I found myself wanting to hurry into the kitchen, where surely Aunt Charlie would have a cup of tea waiting for me. It didn't feel scary at all. It felt warm and comforting.

Like coming home.

How could this be?

Stefan was still muttering under his breath. "I can't believe all this crap. We're going to have put our stuff in storage for months while we go through it all. Christ, like we need another bill to worry about." He sighed, pulled his cell phone out, and started punching numbers.

"Dad, what do you mean our stuff is going into storage?" Chrissy said, clearly alarmed.

Stefan waved his arms. "Honey, look around you. Where are we going to put it? We have to put our things into storage until we get all this out of here."

"But Dad," Chrissy protested. I stopped listening. I walked slowly around, watching my aunt dashing down the stairs, her smock stained, arms filled with herbs and flowers, some even sticking out of her frizzy brown hair, muttering about the latest concoction she was crafting for one of the neighbors whose back was acting up again ...

"Earth to Rebecca. Rebecca. Are you okay?" I suddenly realized Stefan was talking to me, and I pulled myself out of my memories.

"Sorry, it just ..." my voice trailed off.

He came closer. "Are you okay? Are you remembering?"

There she was again, the ghost of Aunt Charlie, explaining yet again to the odd, overly-made-up, hair-over-teased, forty-something woman from the next town that no, she didn't do love potions. It was dangerous magic to mess around with either love or money, but if she wanted help with her thyroid that was clearly not working the way it should be, that was definitely in my aunt's wheelhouse.

I shook my head. "No, not really. It's just ... weird."

I wanted him to dig deeper, ask me questions, invite me to talk about the memories flooding through me. I wanted him to look at me while I spoke, *really* look at me, the way he did before we were married.

Where had it all gone wrong? And how could he leave me alone in a lonely, isolated and desolate house a thousand miles away from New York? Sure, Chrissy would be there, but the jury was still out as to whether she made it better or worse. The memories pushed up against me, smothering me. I *needed* to talk about them, before they completely overwhelmed and suffocated me. And he knew it—he knew how much I needed to talk things through to keep the anxiety and panic at bay. He wouldn't let me down, not now, when I really needed him.

Would he?

It Began With a Lie - Chapter 2

The empty coffee pot mocked me.

It sat on the table, all smug and shiny, its cord wrapped tightly around it.

I had been so excited after unearthing it that morning—yes! Coffee! God knew I needed it.

The night before had been horrible, starting with the fights. I ended up in the living room, where I spent the night on the couch, a cold washcloth draped over my face in a feeble attempt to relieve the mother of all headaches.

Several times, I'd have just dozed off when the sound of Chrissy's footsteps would jerk me awake, as she paced up and down the upstairs hallway. I couldn't fathom what was keeping her up, so finally, after the fourth or fifth time of being woken up, I went upstairs to check on her. She must have heard me on the stairs, because all I saw was of the trail of her white nightgown as she disappeared into her room. I stood there for a moment, wondering if I should go talk to her, but the stabbing pain in my head drove me back downstairs to the safety of the couch and washcloth. I just couldn't face another argument then, in the middle of the night.

She must have decided to stay in her room after that, because I finally drifted off, only waking when the sun shone through the dirty living room window, illuminating all the dust motes floating in the air.

Coffee was exactly what I needed. Except ... I had no beans to put in the coffeemaker. Not that it mattered, I realized after digging through the third box in frustration. I didn't have any cream or sugar either.

Well, at least my headache was gone, although what was left was a weird, hollow, slightly-drugged feeling. Still, I'd take that over the headache any day.

I sighed and rubbed my face. The whole move wasn't starting off very well. In fact, everything seemed to be going from bad to worse, including the fight with Stefan.

"Do you really need to leave?" I asked him again as I followed him to the door. He had just said goodbye to Chrissy, who had immediately disappeared upstairs, leaving us alone. I could see the taxi he had called sitting in the driveway and my heart sank. A part of me had hoped to talk him out of going, but with the taxi already there the possibility seemed even more remote.

He sighed. I could tell he was losing patience. "We've been through this. You know I have to."

"But you just got here! Surely you can take a few days—a week maybe—off to help us unpack and get settled."

He picked up his briefcase. "You know I can't. Not now."

"But when? You promised you would set it up so that you could work from here most of the time. Why can't you start that now?" I could tell his patience was just about gone, but I couldn't stop myself.

He opened the door. A fresh, cool breeze rushed in, a sharp contrast to the musty, stale house. "And I will. But it's too soon. There are still a few things I need to get cleaned up before I can do that. You know that. We talked about this."

He stepped outside and went to kiss me, but I turned my face away. "Are you going to see *her*?"

That stopped him. I could see his eyes narrow and his mouth tighten. I hadn't meant to say it; it just slipped out.

He paused and took a breath. "I know this whole situation has been tough on you, so I'm going to forget you said that. I'll call you."

Except he didn't. Not a single peep in the more than twelve hours since he had walked out the door. And every time I thought of it, I felt sick with shame.

I didn't *really* think he was cheating on me. I mean, there was something about Sabrina and her brittle, cool, blonde, perfect elegance that I didn't trust, but that wasn't on Stefan. I had no reason not to trust him. Just because my first husband cheated on me didn't mean Stefan would. And just because Sabrina looked at Stefan like he was a steak dinner, and she was starving, didn't mean it was reciprocated.

Worse, I knew I was making a bigger mess out of it every time I brought it up. The more I accused him, the more likely he would finally say, "Screw it, if I'm constantly accused of being a cheater, I might as well at least get something out of it." Even knowing all of that, I somehow couldn't stop myself.

Deep down, I knew I was driving him away. And I hated that part of myself. But still nothing changed.

To make matters worse, it didn't take long after Stefan left before things blew up with Chrissy. I asked her to help me start organizing the kitchen, and she responded with an outburst about how much she hated the move. She hated me, too—her life was ruined, and it was all my fault. She stormed off, slammed the door to her room, and that's how I ended up on the couch, my head pounding, wishing I was just about anywhere else.

Standing in the kitchen with the weak sunlight peeking through the dirty windows, the empty coffee maker taunting me, I gave in to my feelings of overwhelm. How on earth was I ever going to get the house organized? And the yard? And my aunt's massive garden? All the while researching what it would take to sell the house for top dollar, and dealing with Chrissy? My heart sank at that thought, although I wasn't completely sure which thought triggered it. Maybe it was all of them.

And if that wasn't difficult enough, I also had to deal with being in my aunt's home. Her presence *was everywhere*. I felt like an intruder. How could I do all of this, feeling her around me? How could I be in her home, when she wasn't? It wasn't my house. It was Aunt Charlie's. And I wasn't even sure I WANTED it to feel like my home.

Because if it did, then I would probably remember everything.

Including what happened that night.

The night I almost died.

God, I felt sick.

I needed coffee. And food.

Maybe I should take Chrissy out for breakfast as a peace offering. We could get out of the house, which would be good for me at least, and then go grocery shopping before coming home to tackle the cleaning and organizing.

I wanted to start in the kitchen. It was Aunt Charlie's favorite room in the house, and I knew it would have broken her heart to see how neglected and dingy it had become. When my aunt was alive, it was the center of the home—a light, cheery place with a bright-red tea kettle constantly simmering away on low heat on the stove. Oh, how Aunt Charlie loved her tea—that's why the kettle always had hot water in it—she'd say you just never knew when a cup would be needed. She was a strong believer that tea cured just about everything, just so long as you had the right blend. And, surprise, surprise, you could pretty much always find the right blend outside in her massive garden, which I had no doubt was completely overgrown now. I didn't have the heart to go look.

I could almost see her, standing in that very kitchen, preparing me a cup. "Headache again, Becca?" she would murmur as she measured and poured and steeped. The warm fragrance would fill the homey kitchen as she pushed the hot cup in front of me, the taste strong, flavorful, and sweet, with just a hint of bitterness. And, lo and behold, not too long after drinking it, I would find my headache draining away.

I wondered if I would still find her tea blends in the kitchen. Maybe I could find that headache tea. And maybe, if I was even luckier, I would find a blend that would cure everything that ailed me that morning.

With some surprise, I realized just how much love encompassed that memory. Nothing scary. Nothing that could possibly foretell the horror of what happened that dreadful night.

Could my aunt actually be the monster?

My mother certainly thought so. She forbade any contact, any mentioning of my aunt even, refusing to allow her to see me once I woke up in intensive care following the stomach pump.

She refused her again when I was transferred to a psych unit, after becoming hysterical when I was asked what had happened that night.

My mother blamed my aunt.

And, I, in my weakened, anxious, panicked state, was relieved to follow her lead. Actually, I was more than relieved; I was happy, too.

But sitting in that kitchen right then, I felt only love and comfort, and I began to question my choices.

My mother had been completely against us moving back here, even temporarily. At the time, listening to her arguments, I had chalked it up to her being overly protective. Now, I wondered. Was that it? Or was something deeper going on?

Chrissy chose that moment to stroll into the kitchen, her hair sticking up on one side. She was wearing her blue and red plaid sleep shorts and red tee shirt—the blue plaid almost an exact match to the blue highlight in her hair. Staring at her, something stirred deep inside me—a distinct feeling of wrongness … of something being off—but when I reached for it, I came up empty.

She leaned against the counter and started checking her iPhone. "How sweet, you're being domestic."

I shook my head—that off feeling still nagged at me, but I just couldn't place it. I really needed coffee. Coffee would make everything better.

She tapped at her iPhone, not looking up. "Anything to eat in this God-awful place?"

I sighed. Maybe I should be looking for a tea that would cure Chrissy.

More *Charlie Kingsley Mysteries:*
A Grave Error (a free prequel novel)
The Murder Before Christmas (Book 1)
Ice Cold Murder (Book 2)
Murder Next Door (Book 3)
The Murder of Sleepy Hollow (Book 5)
Red Hot Murder (Book 6)
A Cornucopia of Murder (Book 7)
A Room for Murder (Book 8)
A Wedding to Murder For (novella)
Loch Ness Murder (novella)

Secrets of Redemption *series:*
It Began With a Lie (Book 1)
This Happened to Jessica (Book 2)
The Evil That Was Done (Book 3)
The Summoning (Book 4)
The Reckoning (Book 5)
The Girl Who Wasn't There (Book 6)
The Room at the Top of the Stairs (Book 7)
The Search (Book 8)
The Secret Diary of Helen Blackstone (novella)

The Redemption Detective Agency series:
The Mysterious Case of the Missing Motive (Book 1)

Standalone books:
Today I'll See Her (novella)
The Taking
The Third Nanny
Mirror Image
The Stolen Twin

Access your free exclusive bonus scenes from *A Cornucopia of Murder* right here:
MPWNovels.com/r/q/corn-bonus

Acknowledgements

It's a team effort to birth a book, and I'd like to take a moment to thank everyone who helped.

My writer friends, Hilary Dartt and Stacy Gold, for reading early versions and providing me with invaluable feedback. My wonderful editor, Megan Yakovich, who is always so patient with me. My designer, Erin Ferree Stratton, who has helped bring my books to life with her cover designs.

And, of course, a story wouldn't be a story without research, and I'm so grateful to my friends who have so generously provided me with their expertise over the years: Dr. Mark Moss, Andrea J. Lee, and Steve Eck. Any mistakes are mine and mine alone.

Last but certainly not least, to my husband Paul, for his love and support during this sometimes-painful birthing process.

About Michele

A USA Today Bestselling, award-winning author, Michele taught herself to read at 3 years old because she wanted to write stories so badly. It took some time (and some detours) but she does spend much of her time writing stories now. Mystery stories, to be exact. They're clean and twisty, and range from psychological thrillers to cozies, with a dash of romance and supernatural thrown into the mix. If that wasn't enough, she posts lots of fun things on her blog, including short stories, puzzles, recipes and more, at MPWNovels.com.

Michele grew up in Wisconsin, (hence why all her books take place there), and still visits regularly, but she herself escaped the cold and now lives in the mountains of Prescott, Arizona with her husband and southern squirrel hunter Cassie.

When she's not writing, she's usually reading, hanging out with her dog, or watching the Food Network and imagining she's an awesome cook. (Spoiler alert, she's not. Luckily for the whole family, Mr. PW is in charge of the cooking.)

Made in the USA
Monee, IL
30 November 2023